HER REAL-LIFE
HERO

HER REAL-LIFE HERO

BY

TRISH WYLIE

MILLS & BOON®

For Alfie, the family and all its extensions…
for always being there.

*First published in Great Britain 2004
Large Print edition 2005
Harlequin Mills & Boon Limited,
Eton House, 18-24 Paradise Road,
Richmond, Surrey TW9 1SR*

© Trish Wylie 2004

ISBN 0 263 18554 0

*Set in Times Roman 16 on 17½ pt.
16-0505-49688*

*Printed and bound in Great Britain
by Antony Rowe Ltd, Chippenham, Wiltshire*

CHAPTER ONE

*JACK LEWIS stood in her doorway, the rain run-
ning in silvery rivulets across the broad expanse
of his chest. With his damp shirt still in her
hand, Catherine finally remembered to take a
deep breath into her air-starved lungs.*

*He took her breath away. Never before had
she felt so very feminine, in the most basic
sense. With his presence dominating the small
space of the captain's cabin she suddenly felt
vulnerable, small.*

'You're staring.'

*She blinked at him, swallowing to moisten her
dry throat. 'Am I?'*

*Jack smiled slowly, his eyes hooded as he ob-
served her flushed cheeks. 'You like what you
see, Lady Catherine?'*

*Catherine stared into darkened eyes. 'And if
I do?'*

*She was surprised by her own daring, by the
transformation from well-bred lady to wanton
woman. When had that happened? Had she
lived so sheltered an existence for so long that*

5

the need for a man was overshadowing all her morals and values? But then she doubted the need would have been half so great had Jack been an elderly duke with a paunch. The man was, quite simply, beautiful—from the tousled hair that fell across his forehead to the deep blue eyes that heated her blood as they moved their gaze slowly across her.

He moved closer to her. Then closer still, his eyes steady as he gave a slow, sensual smile. 'Would you like to see more?'

Her dove-grey eyes blinked at him, her breathing a series of short gasps that pressed her breasts against the confines of her tightly laced corset.

'Tell me what it is you want.'

The rain pounded against the windows of the cabin, the wind rocking the floor beneath their feet. The winter storm was as fierce in its intensity as the need that grew low in her stomach. Just one night. One night to live out every fantasy she'd ever had but would never confess to. Would she be damned for ever for taking that night and making it a memory that she could carry for the rest of her life?

'I want you to kiss me.'

He smiled. 'Is that all you want me to do?'

She threw his shirt aside, glancing back at his chest. 'I can choose?'

He reached out one long finger and raised her chin until her eyes met his. Then he closed the final distance between them so that she could feel the heat of his body against her. 'We can do whatever you desire, Lady Catherine. There is no world of control and etiquette here to hold you from your deepest desires.'

She eddwqpmfpppppppf .vvvves[[[[[[[[

'For crying out loud, Percival, get off my keyboard!'

The large tabby blinked at her in annoyance as Tara shooed him off the desk. She knew it had to be eight o'clock. Percival always had dinner at eight o'clock, regardless of whether or not his owner was in the middle of a rather steamy chapter.

'All these years struggling to be a successful writer and I still get dictated to by a feline whose greatest joy is a dead mouse.' She smiled indulgently at the rotund beast. 'Well, so much for passion this evening, then.'

Grinning at the image she presented in the dark reflection of the picture window at her side, Tara stood up and bowed. 'Another glamorous evening in the life of writer Tara Devlin. While she freshens her ageing thirty-year-old skin with a rather good lemon face pack, she is dressed in the best of worn-out towelling robes and the comfort in footwear that can only be found with reindeer slippers. Once again—' she twirled in front of the window, placing a hand on her hip to pose as she pouted '—Tara is sporting the very latest in hairstyles, with an interesting en-semble of both foam *and* Velcro rollers. The epitome of romance in this day and age, Tara is single and almost of spinster age. She remains optimistic at heart, but has about as much chance of meeting an eligible male as she has of being the first female to live on the moon. Ladies and gentlemen—and felines—I give you—and please feel free to take her, because she's obviously been living on her own for too long—Tara Devlin!' She bowed low.

There was a loud knock on her front door.

'Aha!' Upright, she placed both hands on her hips and jumped one hundred and eighty de-grees, Batman-style. 'What handsome stranger has come to whisk me away from this solitude?'

The cat watched her indulgently as she bounced to the doorway.

Stopping in front of the heavy oak, she straightened her robe and swung the door open. The rain-soaked man immediately stepped in past her, shaking his head before he turned to look at her. Then he stared, blinking his blue, blue eyes.

Tara blinked back at him.

He studied her, from her lemon face to her reindeer-clad feet, before raising his eyebrows and smiling. 'Is this a bad time?'

She continued staring. *Him.* There he was, right there, larger than life, in her house. Was it Christmas already? What a gift. Water dripped from his rapidly spiking hair, catching her attention. It was raining? Well, that explained her recent meanderings on the computer.

He waved a large hand in front of her face. 'Hello?'

'I'm guessing either it's raining or you just went swimming fully clothed.' She glanced out through the doorway before closing the door. No jolly man in red.

'Oh...' He shook his head again, dislodging more droplets of water. 'It's raining, all right. You didn't hear it? It's definitely Ark-building weather.'

'No. I was…' She looked towards her computer and searched for words. She could hardly tell him exactly what she'd been writing. 'I was preoccupied.'

He followed her gaze to the desk by the window. 'Surfing the net, were you?'

'Not quite.' She grinned. The grin froze on her face as she felt the tightening of skin around her mouth and nose. She wasn't actually standing talking to *him*, the object of all her recent fantasies, while still wearing a face pack? 'Oh, well—damn.'

'Excuse me?'

'I must look like the creature from the green lagoon.'

He laughed, a deeply masculine sound that vibrated the air between them. 'Well, it is an interesting shade. I like the slippers, though.'

'Oh, dear God.'

'It's all right, I'm sure you weren't expecting some guy to knock on your door.'

She glanced down from his smiling face, noting the straight white teeth and wide lower lip along the way. Was he actually more gorgeous up close? Tall, broad, long legs—pretty darn well put together, actually, in an 'all-male' sort of way. A rare thing. She glanced back up at his face and blushed beneath her mask as she realised he was watching her silent perusal. 'So, I take it you're lost?'

A knowing smile crossed his mouth. 'You can tell that from your studying, can you?'

'Well, you must be to be out here at this time of night. In the rain.'

'I'm not lost. I'm right where I should be.'

'Really? Right here, dripping water on my floor, is where you should be?'

'Not quite.' He held out his hand to her. 'I'm your neighbour.'

She blinked, pretending she really didn't know. 'You're kidding? You bought that wreck next door? Are you mad?'

He seemed amused as she held her hand out for him to shake.

'Something like that. I like fixer-uppers.'

Tara smiled. 'Then you bought the right house. I'm Tara Devlin, and I don't normally look like this.'

'I'm now intrigued to know what you do look like.' He continued to hold her hand in his. 'And for some reason...' He glanced down over the curved outline of her robe, returning the earlier perusal she'd made of him. 'I don't think I'll be disappointed when I know.'

Tara snatched her hand from his, drawing the lapels of her robe closer together. 'You must have X-ray vision if you can see through this thing.'

'I have an instinct for these things.'

'I'll just bet you do.' Oh, yes, indeed; she'd heard the rumours about him already. She frowned slightly, wrinkling the face pack to such an extent that she was sure she must look like an eighty-year-old. 'So, is there a reason for this visit? Or did you just drop by to test out your intuition?'

He smiled sheepishly. 'Much as I would like to say I was being neighbourly, I'm afraid it's simpler and more selfish than that. My Jeep has broken down. I need to call a mechanic or I can't get working tomorrow.'

'No phone?'

'No, it's not connected in the house yet.' One hand disappeared into the pocket of his heavy jacket and produced a mobile phone. 'And there wouldn't appear to be very good reception here.'

Tara studied the top of his head for a moment as he looked down at his phone. He glanced up at her and their eyes locked again. Then he grinned, the dimples in his cheeks reappearing. 'So, do you think I can use your phone?'

She continued to stare at him. He really was sexy…from a writer's point of view, of course. Not a pretty boy, but attractive in a chunky kind of way. Thick knitted sweater, worn jeans, heavy walking boots and all. She wondered if his sweater was at all damp, and her mind wandered back to the work on her computer screen, her mouth suddenly going quite dry…

'Tara?'

Her pulse jumped at the low sound of her name on his lips. Dear Lord, when had her name got so sexy? Her eyes focused on his mouth entirely of their own accord. She shook her head to clear her mind.

'The phone's over there.'

He followed the direction of her pointing finger. Stepping closer to the phone, he was only slightly surprised to find he was going to have to hold Tweety Pie to his ear as he spoke. He glanced over his shoulder. 'Uh, thanks.'

Tara continued to watch him as he read the number from his mobile phone, dialling it into the cartoon character's belly. Already she was continuing the scene from her book in her head, mentally picturing him as the hero—yet again.

It had obviously been way too long since she'd been on a date.

'Hello, McIlvenna's? Yeah, my Jeep has died on the Coast Road and I was wondering if you could pick it up for me?' He turned to smile over his shoulder at Tara. 'Yeah, half an hour's fine. I'll meet you down there.'

Tara smiled feebly as he looked back towards the picture window and the rain sweeping against it.

'That's great. Yeah. You need a name?' His eyes found hers again. 'It's Lewis, Jack Lewis.'

'*What* did you just say your name was?'

Jack set Tweety Pie back into Sylvester's grasp and turned to look at the alien lady. She really was quite…unusual. He'd come to think she didn't exist since he'd moved into his house. Only a light on into the small hours of the morning betrayed the fact that he actually had a neighbour.

'Sorry, I should have said. My name's Jack.'

'Jack Lewis?'

'Yes.' He smiled. 'Shouldn't you go take that stuff off your face? My sisters always say that they get this big blotchy red rash when they leave it on too long.'

She continued staring. 'No. Just let me get this straight in my head. Your name is Jack Lewis and your *Jeep* just broke down on the Coast Road?'

Jack blinked for a moment and then made the major decision to play along. Rather than calling the local mental health institute.

'Yes, and yes. Is that significant in some way?'

'You can't be, you see.' Her laughter sounded vaguely manic, even to her own ears. 'It's just not possible.'

'Which part?'

Her large dove-grey eyes, the one feature he could actually see clearly, blinked at him. 'Any of it. Because I made you up. You're a figment of my imagination. There's just no way you can be—' she blushed beneath her face pack '—*him.*'

She waved her hand towards the computer screen as she spoke, avoiding his direct stare. Jack's eyes followed the movement. He found himself looking at a large tabby cat.

'Nice cat.' Jack hated cats.

'This is a practical joke, right? Who put you up to this?'

'No joke—really.' He aimed his most sincere look at her. 'I really am Jack Lewis. I have been my entire life, since my parents gave me the name. And I do own a Jeep. A blue one. And I don't know what you're talking about. Haven't a clue. But, hey, thanks for the use of your phone.'

He began walking towards the doorway. The rain was suddenly looking pretty darn appealing. The crazy alien lady stepped in front of him.

'How old are you?'

'Thirty-one.'

'Okay, that's right so far.' She seemed to think for a moment, then she folded her arms across her chest and smiled. 'Okay, then, smart guy, how many sisters have you got?'

Jack raised an eyebrow. 'Four?'

'No way!' She stamped a reindeer-clad foot, the action pointless as the soft footwear muffled the sound. 'How could you know that?'

He leaned his head to one side, to look at the door just a few steps behind her left ear. He could make a run for it. After all, he'd played basketball once or twice so he knew how to duck and dive.

'Have you read my manuscript?'

'Your what?'

'My manuscript! Did Eleanor give the synopsis to you?'

'Look, Miss—' He stepped to the right and took a pace forward. 'I don't know anyone called Eleanor. Unless you count my great-aunt, and she's eighty-two and lives in Galway, so I'm going to assume you don't mean her.'

Tara stepped in time with him, still blocking his way. 'That's it, isn't it? She put you up to this to put some of that damned excitement into my life that she's always talking about.'

He watched cautiously as a thought crossed her expressive eyes.

'Are you some kind of gigolo?'

Jack spluttered. 'What?'

'You know, a male pros—'

'Oh, I know what it is!'

'Did she hire you to...to?' She swallowed convulsively, a throbbing pulse beating at the base of her neck. 'Well—to...you know.'

His eyes were drawn to the pulse, the flush that was creeping across her skin. He also noticed how the lapels of her robe were separating to reveal a wide expanse of creamy flesh and the soft rounded edges of her breasts. His body tightened, as much at the innuendo in her words as to the sight of what he was sure must be very naked skin. His eldest sister was right. He needed to get out and about more. Maybe he should actually have looked into some of the many offers he'd had since he'd moved in next door.

'Why don't you tell me, Tara?' His eyes raised once again to clash with hers. 'You seem to know more about me than I do. What have I been hired to do to you, exactly?'

Tara's eyes widened; her voice choked. 'I think you should leave.'

Jack stepped closer to her. 'When I've been hired to—what? Seduce you? Is that what it is?'

She stepped back, her hand reaching behind her for the door handle. 'Jack Lewis wouldn't seduce me.'

Another raised eyebrow. 'Why not?'

'Well, because.'

He smiled at the mature answer. 'Because why?'

Tara found herself backed into the closed door, her eyes still transfixed on the blue of Jack's as her brain searched rapidly for a reason. 'Because I'm not his type.'

'What's his type, then?'

'Beautiful women.' She felt for the door handle. 'Petite, confident, elegant women with—well, with sex appeal.'

Jack smiled. 'Says who? Maybe he—*I* like pretty women with a brain, personality and a wacky sense of humour.'

'You aren't Jack Lewis.'

'Yes, I am.'

'No, you're not.'

He sighed. 'Okay. But please believe me when I tell you that no one sent me here. Yours is the only other doorway for a mile and a half and your lights were on. I am not part of some great conspiracy to get you laid.'

Tara glared at him. 'I beg your pardon?'

'Well, someone obviously thinks you need to get laid pretty badly if you think they'd set you up with a gigolo.'

She continued to glare. 'I do not need to get laid!'

'Really?' He glanced back into the room. 'You live on your own in the middle of nowhere with a cat. And on a Saturday evening you're doing your face and your hair in your comfiest clothes. That shouts single to me.'

'Just who do you think you are to talk to me like that?'

His broad shoulders shrugged nonchalantly. 'You don't believe me when I say who I am, so is there much point trying?'

'Why, you—' She glared at him, lost for words.

'I'm right, aren't I?' Jack grinned, stepping closer to her. 'When's the last time you had sex?'

Her fingers closed around the door handle while she did her best impersonation of a goldfish. Then with rising temper she yanked on it, unintentionally flinging herself towards him as the door opened. His hands reached up to grasp her upper arms as she thudded against his chest.

'Really—' he couldn't resist a taunt '—you don't need to throw yourself at me.'

She struggled against him, setting her small hands on his chest to push him away. 'You are one arrogant—!' she spluttered, then yelled, 'Get out of my house!'

Releasing her, he watched as she gathered her lapels tightly inside one small fist while pointing at the open doorway with her other hand. 'I mean it. Whatever the hell your name is, I want you to leave—right now!'

Jack frowned down at her, realising he'd gone too far. 'Look, we're getting off to a bad start here. We're neighbours, so don't you think we should at least try to—?'

'Out!'

He shook his head, 'Okay—fine. Have it your way.' He stepped out through the doorway before turning to look back at her as the door closed in his face. With a deep breath he yelled through the solid oak, 'You're a nutcase—you know that?'

Tara refused point-blank to allow her new neighbour to irritate her. He could pretend to be a fictional character if he wanted to. She had better things to do with her time. The fact that she'd spent the two weeks since his arrival ogling him out of her window while he laboured away at his rundown house had nothing at all to do with anything. And there were, after all, bound to be some similarities between her hero and the arrogant lump next door. What with her character being based on him...

But the general topic of his arrival was hard to avoid. Especially, as it turned out, in the tiny post office-cum-grocery shop that served the very rural community of Ross's Point, population twenty-two and two-thirds—Mrs Dalgety's eldest daughter being six months gone.

Tara spent an inordinately long amount of time loitering there between the grocery shelves. It wasn't her fault she couldn't find the particular brand of soup that she really wanted. It also wasn't her fault that people talked loudly in the shop. It was unintentional eavesdropping. Honestly.

'And I hear he's *definitely* not married, y'know.' Mrs Donnelly folded her arms across her ample chest, nodding her head knowingly at her audience. 'You'd have thought a man like that would have a nice wife by his age. Do you think he's one of those *happy* men?'

Tara smirked. Gay, had she meant? Oh, she bet he'd love that.

Mrs McHugh raised an eyebrow below her perfectly curled grey hair. 'Geraldine Donnelly, you think everyone is one of those if they're not married by the time they turn thirty.'

'Well,' the well-rounded woman huffed, 'it's just not natural, is all. Why isn't he married by now? There has to be a reason. And sure there's our Philomena, not married and only ten miles away.'

And about five stone overweight if Tara's memory served.

Sheila Mitchell, Tara's closest neighbour bar the obvious one, and the only person even vaguely close to her age, smiled indulgently from behind the counter. 'Now, ladies, don't you think it might just be a case of the man not having found the right woman for him yet?'

Both women glared at her. 'And why not, may I ask?' Edith McHugh demanded. 'Sure, and what's wrong with him if his family hasn't found him a nice girl before now? He even took our Fiona's number, don't you know? And he never bothered calling her. A nice girl like that would have done him lovely.'

Sheila continued, smiling calmly, 'It's true it's not that easy to find a nice girl these days. There aren't just so many of us about any more. Maybe he didn't phone because he was busy.'

'There's such a thing as manners, Sheila. Philomena asked him for dinner and he hadn't even the courtesy to give her an answer. I've heard he's been talking to nearly every single woman hereabouts, and not one of them has he bothered to walk out with. It's just not right at his age. *You* were married by the time you turned twenty-four, Sheila. Late enough in my opinion.' Geraldine bristled. 'Much older than that in my day and age and you'd have been an aged spinster. *Nobody* would have took you on.'

Three pairs of eyes swept in Tara's general direction. Tara glanced up and smiled weakly. 'Ladies.'

Edith sighed. 'No slight intended, you understand, Tara.'

She gritted her teeth slightly. 'Of course not.' Then, dropping to her haunches to examine the bottom shelf, she lowered her voice. 'Nasty old—'

Sheila's voice rose. 'Have *you* been charmed by our new neighbour yet, then?'

Slowly rising to her full height again, Tara lifted an eyebrow. *'Me?'*

Join the queue of women he'd been standing up all over the country? Uh-uh. She'd stick with the men in her books, if it was all the same, thank you. Much safer. Less involved. No broken hearts in Tara's house beyond the ones she created and then mended...

Sheila grinned and the other women watched carefully, their eyes moving backwards and forwards between the younger two. 'Yes, you. Jack Lewis? You live closest to him of all of us. So have you met him yet?'

Tara could feel her cheeks warming slightly. Great—that would help the slight rash she had from wearing her face pack for twice the suggested time.

'Are we quite sure his name is what he says he it is?'

Geraldine Donnelly harrumphed loudly. 'Well, I'd think that Sheila would know his name better than anyone else. She's postmistress after all. She needs to make sure of these things in case of fraud or deception. Don't you, Sheila?'

'Well, I did see his driver's licence as identification when he first signed a cheque for the shop.' Sheila glanced apologetically towards Tara. 'It's the rules. We have to see something with a photograph the first time. You wouldn't believe the number of con artists that flit through here in the summer. So we have to be careful.'

'Of course you do, Sheila.'

'Desperate times altogether.'

The eyes returned to study Tara again. Tara glanced at each in turn, then looked steadily at Sheila. 'And you're quite sure it said Jack Lewis?'

'Oh, yes.'

She frowned. 'Right.'

'So, have you met him, then?'

She nodded, her eyes sweeping back to the tin in her hand. 'He stopped by. Have you any—uh—tomato soup?'

'On your left, second shelf down. So when did he ''stop by''? Was it a social visit?'

Tara set down the mushroom soup and located the tomato. 'His Jeep broke down and he needed to phone McIlvenna's to collect it.'

Sheila watched her study the soup tin intently. 'Is that right? And what did you think of him?'

Tara set the tin into the crook of her arm and lifted a loaf of bread, her eyes still avoiding Sheila's. 'Well, I didn't really speak to him for long, y'know. I'm sure he's very biddable.' She lowered her voice to mumble, 'Ordinarily.'

'And definitely single, we hear.' Edith emphasised the word 'single' with a raise of her eyebrow. 'Not that bad-looking that you couldn't look at him over the breakfast table either.'

Sheila laughed, Geraldine stared in shock, and Tara went the same colour as the soup advertised on her tin. 'I'm sure I didn't notice, Mrs McHugh. After all, I'm well known for being very content as a spinster.'

Stepping up to the counter, she offered Sheila the necessary money, smiling with gritted teeth as she waited for her change.

'That man seemed more than capable of getting breakfast on his own.'

Sheila smiled softly, bobbing her head lower to catch Tara's eye. 'Never worry yourself, Tara. The ladies mean no harm. I'm sure he'll be a fine neighbour for you. It'll be nice for you to have another friend close to your age. Just watch he doesn't go standing you up, same as Fiona and Philomena. If it goes anywhere, though, you'd be more than welcome to bring him to lunch on Sunday. We could make a day of it.'

Oh, yeah, that was likely. She blinked for a moment. 'I'm sure he's very busy with his work. It'll take a bulldozer to put that place back the way it used to look.' Tara glanced sideways at the others. 'And I doubt he's the lonely kind, or he wouldn't have been so rude to Fiona and Philomena.'

'Well, if you change your mind….'

'Thanks, Sheila.' She glanced back over her shoulder as she left the store, her ears burning before she'd even passed the gable wall. Wicked old gossips. She wondered how her friend put up with them without committing mass murder.

Turning onto the narrow path that led out of the tiny village, along the edge of the cliffs and back to her small house overlooking the bay, Tara smiled. Nothing ever seemed bad for too long on this kind of a day. The clear sky spread wide and far above her head, with only a hint or two of candyfloss clouds. And the sea, reflecting the same blue, was rolling into the bay, its white crests high as the offshore breeze tried to push the waves back. It was awe-inspiring. It was the main reason why Tara stayed at Ross's Point to write.

As she came closer to her summer house she had to pass by the fixer-upper that Jack Lewis had bought. It had been a lovely house once upon a time, but years of neglect and the onslaught of its coastal position had taken their toll on the Victorian building. She stopped to look up at the house, closing her eyes for a moment as she imagined how it had looked when it was loved and cared for. With a small smile she then turned towards her own smaller house, which was still much loved and cared for. Her haven from the rest of the big, bad world.

From the corner of her eye she caught a flash of red. As she walked past the end of the large house she could see a ladder, and as her eyes moved upwards she could see a man on the ladder. The famous Jack Lewis, no doubt.

She tried not to look. Really she did. She tried not to see how the worn jeans sat low on his behind. She tried really hard not to glance sideways at his back as he reached upwards to fix new guttering to the porch, his red T-shirt stretching and moving with the muscles underneath. And she most definitely didn't notice the way the light caught his hair, teasing out blond streaks amongst the light brown.

It was just so damned ridiculous, this obsession she'd had with him since he'd bought the house. As if she couldn't think of anything else. It was why she'd allowed her imagination to form a plotline round him. Well, her fantasies needed an outlet somewhere…

But the man was quite obviously a piece of work. She'd heard tales linking him with single, available women all over the county since he'd arrived. And not one of those stories had a happy ending that she was aware of.

She noticed how his ladder suddenly wobbled. And she remembered something else.

Chapter Two, page twenty-three. Jack Lewis fell from the ship's rigging and broke his ankle. It was in her manuscript. Just how far was this idiot prepared to go to get her attention?

The ladder wobbled again, the guttering coming loose in his hand. With a loud expletive, the real live Jack Lewis started to fall.

CHAPTER TWO

JACK had seen her coming. In fact he'd seen her leave in the first place. And he'd been caught completely off guard. Who'd have thought it? The mystery neighbour wasn't at all tough on the eyeballs without her lemon face pack and horrid towelling robe. He knew that for a fact now that he'd seen her in snug-fitting jeans and a grey scoop-necked T-shirt, which hugged everywhere it needed to hug.

She had left her small house less than half an hour ago, bowing her head as she followed the path alongside his house. It had irritated him then, and ever since she'd been gone. Was she going to look at her feet every time she walked past him? It was ridiculous. Jack was, after all, a likeable guy. Lots of people said so. Kind to animals and small children and everything.

Guessing that as she'd left on foot she was probably headed for the local shop, he decided that he'd be outside when she returned. That way he could accidentally see her and strike up a conversation, in a neighbourly kind of a way.

And she'd darn well have to be rude to avoid him! After all, he was looking at the guts of a year's work on this house, and she couldn't keep pointedly avoiding him for that long. It would be—well, adolescent.

Add to that the fact that from what he'd seen so far she was the best-looking woman for about twenty miles. And he knew that because he'd had single women introducing themselves ever since he'd arrived. Some days he felt as if he was the only man left on the planet! It was Murphy's Law that the most interesting one didn't want anything to do with him, and it bruised his ego slightly. Everything suggested he try getting to know her again.

Deciding that the porch would be his best position, he'd waited until he could see her in the distance, then he'd sprinted outside to get up the ladder. In his haste he'd managed to forget to set bricks at the base of the ladder, which he normally used to secure it.

He remembered when he got to the top. 'Damn!'

She stopped at the edge of the house, her eyes sweeping upwards. The place must have looked like a complete dump to her, but to Jack it was merely neglected. Someone had loved this house once; it would have been something in its heyday. He intended for it to be *something* again. All it needed was a little of his special attention.

She'd closed her eyes, a small smile crossing her mouth. Jack swallowed hard. Good God, what kind of thought had put that look on her face? Her head tilted slightly, the breeze teasing her shoulder-length blonde hair. Jack thought about giving *her* some of his 'special attention', then forced himself to take a deep, calming breath, leaning out a little further to get a better view.

She opened her eyes and turned to walk towards her house.

Then she just happened to glance in his direction.

He immediately reached forward to play with the guttering. Had she seen him staring? Since when had he become such a voyeur? With a deep breath he decided to look straight at her and simply say hi. But then the ladder wobbled again.

He reached out for a firmer hold. The old guttering gave way. And he headed towards the ground with the grace of a two-ton rhino.

'*Ummphf!*' Damn. The fall had been fine, but the landing hurt like hell.

Tara dropped her bag and ran towards him, 'Are you all right?' She dropped onto her haunches beside him, her hand reaching to brush across his forehead, her fingers gently searching for bumps. 'Are you conscious?'

Mostly of the fact that she was touching him, if truth was told. Her small hands moved downwards, checking his collarbone, across his arms, chest, and down over the bottom half of his legs. He smiled inwardly. She obviously wasn't too concerned that he'd broken anything in between.

'Can you hear me?'

Guilt hit him at the concern in her voice. He opened his eyes.

She blinked down at him, her arched eyebrows raised in question.

Jack smiled slightly. 'Hello, again.'

She smiled back, her eyes softening, 'Hi. Do you hurt anywhere?'

He had an ache in his chest for some reason. Winded, probably. The woman really did have the most amazing eyes—stormy, almost. He continued smiling like an idiot. At least she was speaking to him. Mission accomplished, in a roundabout way.

'I'm fine. At least, I think I am.'

She blushed as he continued to smile up at her. 'Did you hit your head?'

'If I did it's my own stupid fault for not putting the bricks in place. I'm not normally that dumb.'

A mischievous light entered her eyes. 'Really?'

'Really it's my own fault? Or really I'm not normally that dumb?'

'The latter.'

He laughed, pushing himself up onto his elbows. 'Yeah, I thought that's what you meant.' He rubbed a hand across the back of his head, searching for and finding the lump she'd missed while he lay on it. 'Good job I fell on the thickest part of me.'

Her smile was replaced almost immediately with a stern frown as he tried to push himself up onto his feet. 'What do you think you're doing?'

'Something we men have been able to do for a great many centuries now. It's called standing up.'

'I don't think so.'

'Okay, then, what *is* it called?'

She sighed. 'Cute.'

'You think I'm cute? That's not what you said the last time we met.'

Her eyes widened. 'You don't stop doing that, do you?'

'I'm sorry.' He held his hands up in front of him. 'It's a habit of mine. Not everyone likes it, I'll admit. You learn good verbal sparring skills when you have four older sisters. It's a survival thing.'

Tara leaned back slightly, suspicion in her eyes. 'Mmm, I'd imagine so.'

He tried to make polite conversation. 'Do you have brothers or sisters?'

She avoided his steady gaze. 'A brother.'

'Older or younger?'

They looked at each other for a silent moment. Finally Tara stood up. After all, if he could make conversation he obviously wasn't dying. 'Well, if you don't have concussion or anything—'

She was trying to leave. Jack reacted quickly. 'Well, there is just this one bump back here.' He pointed to the back of his head. 'And I am a bit starry-eyed for some reason. But I'm sure it'll pass.'

Tara hesitated, unsure for a moment whether to actually trust him or not. After all, with his reputation…

But then, he had hit the ground rather hard. Mass plus velocity equalled impact, and he was quite a large mass. And she wouldn't be able to live with the guilt if he did have concussion.

Jack watched the uncertainty on her face, the debate that she was obviously having with herself. Then, with a small sigh, she stepped forward and reached down to run her fingers through the hair at the back of his neck. Man, but it felt good. Soothing, almost—except for the small fact that it brought her denim-clad thighs right up close to his face. He averted his eyes. Which, he modestly thought, was chivalrous of him.

While searching the back of his head for any missed lumps, Tara noted the small turn of his head that indicated he wasn't staring at her thighs. With a blink of surprise she accepted that it was vaguely sweet.

There was just no way she could allow herself to discover that he might actually be a nice guy, though. Not when his name was what it was, and most certainly not after the recent wanderings of her imagination. It was just too darn distracting. When she thought of the name she thought about the man she'd created, the man whom mentally she'd already kissed and was about to make love with. The writer had turned herself into the heroine; the woman had already fantasised on many a warm evening alone... Oh, no, too distracting altogether.

Her fingers found the lump. 'You do have a bump, right enough.'

'You think I'd lie?'

She glanced down at his upturned face. 'Would you?'

'To get to talk to you longer?' He smiled sheepishly. 'Probably.'

Ah. There it was. The thing that he'd been doing on all the local girls. 'You can cut that out, you know. It won't wash with me.'

'What won't?'

'Flirting.' Her fingers remained in his short hair as she looked into his eyes. 'I'm immune.'

A wolfish grin appeared. 'You make that sound like a challenge.'

Oh, yes, that was naturally how he'd interpret it, wasn't it? Rolling her eyes heavenwards, she released his head then held out a hand to help him onto his feet. 'Does this approach actually work for you? I mean, do you just keep going until women submit because you've irritated them to breaking point? It's a novel approach.'

He placed his hand in hers but used his other hand to push himself up from the ground. When he was once again towering over her, he smiled down. 'You're very cynical. Has it occurred to you that women might find my jovial nature endearing?'

Tara snorted gracefully. 'I doubt it. An irritating manner doesn't tend to be one of the assets that women look for in men.'

'You'd be an expert on what women look for in men, would you?'

'I have a fairly good idea, yes.' She tried to pull her hand free from his. 'Is that so difficult to believe, me being a woman and all?'

He held her hand a little tighter. 'Are you a sex therapist?' His grin widened. '*Please* tell me you're a sex therapist.'

Despite her best efforts not to, Tara laughed, tugging at her hand again. 'Oh, you'd just love that, wouldn't you? Every man's fantasy after a porno star, right?'

'You're not a—?'

She wagged a free finger at him. 'Don't go there!'

'All right, then, I guess I'll have to downscale my fantasy role models a little to include what you do.' He tugged on her hand, placing it closer to his chest. 'So what do you do, Tara Devlin, that gives you this enviable knowledge of what all women want?'

Another tug at her hand. 'You know what I do.'

'Would I ask if I did? Unless I was really forgetful. Which, incidentally, I doubt very much I *would* be around you. You're proving fairly memorable.'

He really was very good at being charming. 'Would you stop already?'

'Stop what?'

'The flirting thing.' She tugged twice on her hand. 'Seriously.'

'Why?'

Tara wanted to scream. She'd never met anyone so irritating in her entire life. 'Would you give me my damn hand?'

He held on tighter. 'Why?'

Thinking on her feet having always been one of her best traits, Tara stepped closer and slammed her foot down on his.

'Ow!' He released her hand and stepped back, looking down at his soft, well-worn trainers and then at her hiking boots. 'That hurt.'

Tara folded her arms neatly across her chest. 'It was meant to. But I bet it'll take your mind off your sore head.'

His eyebrows jumped upwards, then he roared with laughter. 'I think I'm going to enjoy living next door to you. You're always going to keep me on my toes, aren't you?'

'I have absolutely *no* intention of keeping you on anything.'

'Aw, c'mon, you can't tell me you're not enjoying this just a little?'

She would tell him no such thing. Even if it was the littlest bit true. After all, he was officially the town scoundrel now. And Tara was officially not interested in getting charmed and hurt by the town scoundrel. She'd been hurt a time or two before. That was why she was single.

She *liked* being single.

And then there was the whole name thing. And the whole fantasy thing she had going on in her wee single head. It was all just a little too weird.

Then there was the fall…

'How did you fall off the ladder?'

He blinked at her. 'Gravity?'

'No, you idiot. I mean, what caused it?'

Jack gaped slightly. 'Uh, well, it kind of wobbled and I sort of fell off.' He smiled. 'But gravity helped.'

He was hiding something. Tara knew it—could read it in the way he wouldn't quite look her in the eye. Her eyes narrowed. 'No, there's something else to it, isn't there?'

Jack glanced past her right ear. 'I have no idea what you're talking about.'

'I think you do. So when are you going to tell me who you really are?'

'You know who I really am.' He looked her straight in the eye. 'I thought we'd moved past that. What do you need to believe me? Photo ID?'

'I already know you have photo ID. Sheila in the post office mentioned it.' She shook her head, hair flicking against the edges of her mouth. She reached up and removed a strand that got stuck against her lip. 'But I wrote about you on breaking down on the Coast Road and about your falling down off a ladder—of sorts. Don't you think that's all a bit too weird?'

His blue eyes danced lightly as they looked down at her. He only just managed not to use the 'pot and kettle' analogy. 'So you're a writer. What do you write that foretells the future? Horoscopes?'

Tara blushed. She'd never been embarrassed about what she did for a living. But suddenly, in the presence of this ridiculously sexy man who seemed unable to stop himself from flirting with her, she was uncomfortable. She raised her chin an inch for confidence. 'I write historical adventure, with a romantic edge.'

The edges of his mouth twitched. 'Romance? As in hearts and flowers?'

She glared at him, suddenly defensive. 'No, actually. The romance is sensual in content, if you must know.'

He tried his best to look serious. 'Which means what?'

'Well…' She was digging herself a hole and she damn well knew it. She closed her eyes and took a deep breath. 'It means that the storylines are more relevant to human nature and emotions.' She quoted some of her publisher's publicity material. 'They have heroines and heroes whose experiences a modern-day reader can identify with. And quite often the relationships are reflective of more…more *modern-day* values.'

Jack took a few moments to digest what she'd just told him. Then he started to smile. 'How ''modern-day'' are we talking, here?'

'Meaning?' The hole was getting bigger.

'Well, you and I both know that ''modern-day'' relationships, as you describe them, have a much more *physical* aspect than they did, say, a hundred years ago.'

'Dependent on the morals of the individuals—but yes.'

'So, in order for the romance to be…' Jack searched for the right words '…*realistic,* there has to be an element of…physical contact, right?'

Tara swallowed, wishing that the hole would just swallow her up.

'Yes, there does.'

Jack studied her carefully for a split second, then he grinned widely. 'My word, Miss Tara. You write *sex*, don't you?'

'Oh, get your head out of the gutter, would you?' She spun on her heel, heading back to the path. 'Not everything in this world revolves around the horizontal mambo.'

He fell into step behind her. 'The horizontal *what* was that? I don't believe I've tried that yet. Don't suppose you could describe it for me? Maybe *write* a description out?'

'Get lost!' Tara stopped and swung round to face him, her eyes sparkling angrily. 'You are the single most annoying person I think I've ever met.'

'You should meet more people.'

She shook her head, holding her arms out from her sides. 'I give up.'

'About time too.' He stepped forward, pulled her close to him and kissed her.

How had that happened? Yes, she wrote about this kind of thing every day. But it wasn't something that happened every day in real life. Leastways, not to her.

A complete scoundrel, whose very name was in doubt, was kissing her. Okay, so he was an all-round, physically damned attractive scoundrel, but he was quite obviously a scoundrel nonetheless.

It wasn't as if Tara hadn't kissed men when she didn't know their entire life story, but, hell, she'd known them for more than five minutes before. And she had been kissed by the odd scoundrel before, but she hadn't been forewarned back then. This time she most definitely had, thanks to all the Fionas and Philomenas.

She should have been prepared. His reputation preceded him. This really shouldn't have been such a big surprise.

But the most amazing thing was, if she was going to face up to the truth of the matter, he wasn't doing too bad a job. Not too shabby at all. In fact, her fantasies started to fall a little short…

She stood absolutely still, determined not to participate even as her eyes flickered closed. His mouth moved across hers. Not tentative, but firm—not *too* firm, though. She stopped analysing the experience for future literary use, and instead sensation took over.

Strength. She could feel the overwhelming strength of his body as it enveloped her own. She felt small, vulnerable, and deliciously female.

Musk. Whether it was from his skin or something manufactured, it was heady, sweet. Filling her nostrils with the unfamiliar maleness of his scent.

Sweet-tasting warmth. His mouth opened slightly, his tongue flicking between her lips, encouraging her participation, sending waves of similar sweet warmth throughout her body. *Mmm.*

The moment he felt her soften he smiled in satisfaction against her mouth. The moment he smiled she stiffened and struggled until he let her loose.

With only a glare she turned, lifted her shopping bag, and swung it at his head. It hit the side of his left eye. Immediately he stumbled sideways, before meeting the ground for the second time when his large feet got tangled.

'You arrogant—!'

'What the hell's in that bag?' He lay on his back, both hands held tight against his rapidly swelling eye.

'How dare you kiss me?'

He squinted up at her. 'It seemed like a good idea at the time. What's wrong? Didn't you write that bit?'

'If you ever touch me again I'll call the police—you hear me?' She stood over him, shopping bag swinging. 'I know the local constable and he'll look out for me.'

'I've met the local constable, and unless he's managed to get new glasses he's incapable of looking out for pink elephants, never mind you.'

Jack struggled to his feet. 'Well, if I didn't have concussion before, I've sure as hell got it now.'

Tara failed to notice his slight swaying. 'You can't just go round kissing women who don't want to be kissed!' She watched as he removed his hands from his eye. 'Oh, God.'

He looked at her expression with his one good eye. 'That bad, huh?'

She looked down at the bag and then back at his eye. 'Oh, God.'

'Great. I'm disfigured.' He turned towards the house and tilted dangerously sideways.

'I forgot.' She moved to his side, setting his arm across her shoulders to support him. 'I'm so sorry.'

'You forgot you bought an anvil?'

'No, tomato soup.'

He glanced down at her. 'You just hit me with a tin of soup?'

Tara smiled weakly at him. 'It seemed like a good idea at the time.'

'And *you're* the one calling the police?'

They made it up the porch steps and through the large entrance hall. 'Where to?' Tara glanced from side to side, into large empty rooms with peeling wallpaper and workbenches.

'Kitchen.' He pointed ahead. 'I need an ice pack and possibly a stiff drink.'

He sat down at a worn table while Tara walked to a large fridge. She opened the freezer door, glancing back over her shoulder. 'Peas or sweetcorn?'

'What?' He already had a headache, and she was going nutty on him again.

'You don't have any ice, so do you want frozen peas or sweetcorn?'

'You pick the vegetable. You're good at that.'

She sat opposite him at the table as he placed the bag against his eye. She studied him and guilt kicked in. Even a scoundrel didn't deserve attempted murder. 'I really am sorry I hit you with the tin. But at least the bread cushioned some of the blow, or I'd probably have knocked you out.'

'That's reassuring.'

She attempted to reason. 'But you still shouldn't have kissed me like that.'

Jack sighed. 'Okay, then. How should I have kissed you?'

'You shouldn't have kissed me at all.' She frowned at him, her eyes a mixture of regret and annoyance. 'Not if I didn't ask you to.'

Drips of water began to appear on the edge of the bag as the heat from Jack's eye began to defrost the contents. 'You always *ask* a man to kiss you? Don't tell me. You wear the trousers in all your relationships, right? You give them instructions every step of the way, right from, ''Would you kiss me now?'' through to, ''Do you mind throwing me down and giving me—''?'

The glint of anger in her eyes stopped him. He took a deep breath. 'How about you and I call a truce?'

'What kind of truce?'

Her obvious distrust irritated him, but he continued. 'The kind of truce where we promise not to hit each other with any food, tinned or otherwise, and try to be friends.'

'Friends? You and me?' She shook her head. 'I don't think that would work, to be honest.'

He was beginning to wonder about that himself. 'Why not?'

'We don't get on.'

'How do you know we don't? We haven't tried.'

'I just hit you with a tin of soup!'

'Okay, I'll give you that.' He smiled weakly. 'But you've got to admit life's not boring when we're together.'

One hand reached across to examine the eye below the frozen vegetables. 'Are you willing to risk your other eye?'

'Promise to use mushroom next time?'

She smiled. 'You're crazy.'

'I wouldn't throw stones in that department if I were you.'

'You'd have to promise not to flirt with me.' She leaned back in her chair. 'And you'd have to be less annoying. Think you can manage that?'

'No.'

'Well, then…'

'Flirting is part of my character. It's apparently something I do without thinking.'

'Says who? Your ego?'

'All of my sisters. They've been saying for years it will get me into trouble some day.' He held the bag away from his face. 'And today's that day, it would seem.'

'I really don't see how we can be friends, then.'

He smiled gently, his eyes warming. 'You could try to cure me of it? Or maybe you could just get used to it as you get to know me better?'

She sighed. 'Why do you want to be friends with me?'

A shrug. 'I might just like you. For some unknown reason.'

Tara studied him for several long, silent minutes. Jack stayed quiet, for once. She was curious about him—who he *really* was. What kind of person he might turn out to be below the thick layer of smart-ass. He was right about one thing: life wasn't boring when they were together. And they lived next door to each other. It would be just too awkward if they didn't make some attempt to get along.

For research purposes, maybe? To find out more about what it was like being a scoundrel? She could go with that reasoning. Scoundrels were rife in her writing after all. Research could be a good thing. Especially if she was forearmed. If she already knew he was a scoundrel then she could resist, right? She'd just have to get past the whole ogling thing and limit her fantasising to her fiction.

That all taken into account, there was one thing that sure as hell couldn't happen. 'You can't kiss me again.'

He reached his hand across the table to shake hers. Her smaller hand enclosed in his, he smiled. 'I won't kiss you again. Or do anything else from my wide repertoire.' The smile promoted itself to a grin. 'Until you ask me to.'

CHAPTER THREE

JACK wanted Catherine—had done from the very moment he saw her. She fascinated him, intrigued him, irritated him, challenged him. It was a whirlwind of highs and lows, the biggest adventure of his life.

The storms had come and gone. Their near-lovemaking was an all too recent picture in his memory. Yet in a way he was glad they hadn't made love. Eventually her conscience would have taken the beautiful memory of it and turned it into a moment to regret.

Jack didn't want that to happen.

His eyes hooded, he watched as she moved around the room. She was the centre of attention, all eyes on her in her position as hostess. Beautiful, sparkling, witty, with the right words for everyone.

He didn't want her turning that charm on anyone else but him. He was jealous of a crowded room.

When she finally appeared by his side he lifted one hand to run it along her arm. 'This dress is causing a scandal. You know that, don't you?'

Goosebumps appeared on her skin as the low rumble of his voice touched her ear. His eyes moved slowly over the dress stolen from the Spanish galleon. Everything he said and did had the most profound effect on her, on such a basic and sensual level.

'I think it's perfect.' She glanced down over the revealing red silk before sweeping her gaze upwards over the ruffles of his shirt until finally her eyes locked with his. 'What's so scandalous about it?'

Jack smiled. 'It's what it does to my imagination.'

'And that is?'

'It makes me think about the Captain's cabin, about how much of you I saw, how much of you beneath this dress that I remember, and it makes me—

'Is that the story I'm in?'

Tara jumped at the sound of his voice, then glared across at the open picture window. 'My, what a surprise it is to see you.'

Since she'd seen him every morning for the past week it wasn't that big a surprise, and they both knew it.

Jack grinned. 'Yeah, I missed you, too. So, have I got it yet?'

'Got what, exactly?'

'You know.' He winked at her. *'It.'*

Closing her eyes, she took a deep, calming breath. 'And to think women actually grow out of the ''Ugh—boys'' stage.' She opened her eyes again and smiled sweetly. 'How are you this morning, Mr Romance?'

'All the better for seeing your smiling face.' He stepped in through the window and tried to read over her shoulder. 'How's it going?'

Tara hit the switch on the bottom of her monitor, and the light immediately died on screen. 'Fine. No thanks to you.'

No thanks to him that she'd now tried fifteen different name combinations and none of them were doing it for her. She thought of *her* Jack as the real Jack, and this Jack as the impostor. This one should change his name!

'I've offered to help you out with my insight into the male mind.'

She nodded. 'Oh, I remember. Vividly.'

'Well, I did say that reading your stuff might help my knowledge on the subject.' He tucked her hair behind her ear, grinning down at her. 'Might help me find a chink in your armour.'

He just couldn't stop himself, could he? 'Do you flirt in your sleep?'

'You could find out.'

She laughed involuntarily. 'In your dreams.'

Without thinking he reached up to rub his bad eye. He watched as her eyes followed the movement, a now familiar look of guilt crossing her even features. He smiled, his voice softening. 'It's fine.'

Tara smiled at his tone. He could actually be vaguely nice, when he put his mind to it. When he wasn't being lewd, or argumentative, or any of the other annoying things he was so very practised at being.

'It looks like it hurts like heck.'

He noted the warmth in her eyes and chose the safety of familiar banter. 'Dangerous thing, soup. Except the chicken variety, of course.'

'Don't tell me. Your sweet old mother used to give it to you when you were sick and it made you all better, right?'

'Don't remember.' His gaze moved towards the window.

'You only remember her spitting on a hanky to clean your face outside school while all your friends watched?'

He shrugged, his eyes still on the window. 'Not that bit. The mother bit. She left early on.'

Tara blinked in surprise. 'You're kidding.'

He turned towards her, wearing a smile that didn't quite make it to his eyes. 'Nope, not this time. She decided that a boy was too much to handle after four girls and skipped.'

'No way.'

Jack laughed at her outraged expression. 'Well, maybe not quite as coldly as that, but she did leave when I was about two. I guess the fifth terrible two-year-old was the straw that broke the camel's back. It's no big deal.'

She stared at him. 'You think? I'd have said that it was a pretty big deal.'

Another shrug. 'I'm a big guy now. I've dealt, trust me.'

'I'm sorry.' The words automatically left her lips, seeming inadequate even to her own ears. Something like that could change a person's outlook for ever.

'Did you ask her to leave?'

'No.'

'Well, then, it's hardly your fault, is it?'

'Well, no. But—'

He ruffled her hair. 'Forget it. Help me get paint instead.'

Tara blinked at the sudden change of direction. 'Paint?'

'Yeah—the stuff you plaster onto walls until you can't see the damp patches.' He pointed through the window to his house. 'It needs a lick or two, and since I'm a man—just in case you hadn't noticed already—I'm deemed not to have much taste in paint colours.'

Smoothing down her hair, she smiled at his statement. From a previous conversation she knew this was his fourth house project. 'Who picked the colours before? No, let me guess. You flirt with all your single female neighbours and they pick the colour schemes for you, right?'

Something flickered across his face, then vanished, leaving Tara to wonder if she'd seen anything in the first place.

'Yep, that's it. You have me sussed.' He leaned towards her again, his eyes challenging her as he invaded more and more of her personal space. 'Unless you have something else you'd rather do with the rest of the morning?'

Tara felt her mouth growing dry as his body displaced the air around her. He was just the most *male* male she had ever encountered. It was very disconcerting. She raised her chin defiantly. No wise-ass like him was going to make her go weak at the knees.

With a deep, if somewhat shaky breath, she stared him straight in the eye. 'You know, it's funny, but I just can't think of anything I might do with you that would be more enjoyable than looking at tins of paint.'

Jack thumped his fist against his chest with a dull thud. 'I'm wounded by these constant rejections.'

'You'll live.'

He seemed to consider for a second, then he winked. 'Yeah, you know, I think I will.' Grabbing her hand, he tugged, willing her out of her chair. 'C'mon, you. Come look at paint. Help me out.'

'You're beyond help.'

When she was on her feet he leaned his face towards hers, his warm breath fanning her cheeks, his voice low. 'People in glass houses…'

* * *

The paint store was thirty miles away, so Jack decided to buy lots of paint. And wallpaper. And even though he'd asked Tara for her help he wasn't averse to disagreeing with her choices.

'Not flowers. I'm not having anything with flowers.'

Tara held the sample up in front of his disapproving face. 'It's a very small flower. Tiny, in fact. A woman may well end up living in your house, you know.'

'Not while I'm in it.'

'Well, that goes without saying.'

'What does that mean?'

She turned the sample to look at it again. 'This is really nice wallpaper, Jack. I think it's chic—understated.'

He folded his arms, a frown creasing his forehead. 'No, really, what did that mean? You think no one would want to live with me? I can use utensils and everything. And I'll have you know I'm very lovable.'

Tara laughed. 'Of course you are. Women just drop at your feet. I mean, look at me—I find you completely irresistible.'

'Great.' He took the wallpaper out of her hands and set it back on the rack. 'Then let's go home and do the—what did you call it again?—the horizontal something?'

'Mambo.' She grinned as he made to guide her towards the checkouts. 'But I thought we had paint to buy.'

He stopped and sighed. 'I can't believe you'd rather spend an afternoon looking at wallpaper with flowers on instead of having me guide you to dizzying heights of new-found—'

'I get the picture, thank you.' She blushed furiously, her entire body warm beneath his gaze. How did he keep *doing* that? One minute simply teasing, the next flagrantly trying to coax her into his bed. Did he take anything seriously? It crossed her mind that he could actually turn out to be that famous guy with the notches carved into his bedpost.

'Hello, Jack.'

Tara's eyes were pulled towards the woman in front of them. She was stunning. Absolutely gorgeous. Exactly the kind of woman that the Jack Lewis from her story would have fallen for.

She glanced back at Jack and was amazed by the sudden transformation. The teasing spark she had got to know only too well was gone, replaced instead with a wariness she hadn't seen in him before.

'Sarah.'

'Well, this is a surprise, isn't it?' The woman's dark eyes swept across Tara. 'Aren't you going to introduce me to your friend?'

'No.'

Tara blinked at him, then stretched her hand outwards. 'Tara. And technically we're still working on the friend bit.'

Jack looked at her from the corner of his eye. 'Oh, I'm not a friend of Sarah's either.'

The woman raised an elegant eyebrow. 'There's no need not to be polite, Jack. We've too much history to be snippy, don't you think?'

He thought for a moment, shaking his head. 'No.'

Tara laughed nervously. 'C'mon, Jack—try being nice.'

His eyes swept over to meet Tara's. 'No, and don't *you* try being nice. You two won't be meeting again, trust me.'

While she watched with her mouth gaping he pushed the trolleyful of paint and paper towards the checkout counter.

'He can be irritating sometimes.'

Tara smiled wryly at the younger woman. 'I know. And rude.'

She seemed to study Tara carefully for a moment. 'Tara, right? Are you his latest conquest?'

'Hardly.' She laughed lightly. 'I'm immune to him.'

'He's a terrible flirt.'

'Yeah, I got that part.'

With a glance towards the checkouts Sarah stepped closer to Tara, her voice low. 'Watch yourself with that one. He'll break your heart with his flirting. He just can't stop himself. He's unable to commit.'

'Look, there's really no need for you to tell me this. I'm not—'

'Oh, you will. You'll see. He's never failed to win a woman over. It's a gift.'

Tara found herself disliking the woman, and even Jack a little, for placing her in such an awkward position. 'Really, there's no need to warn me off him. I'm *not* interested. Not that way.'

The woman studied her intently, then looked back at Jack, her expression wistful. 'Just as well for you. I was with him for nearly two years. We even got engaged. And I have to say it caused me nothing but heartbreak.'

Tara stared at her profile in surprise.

'He just couldn't stay away from other women. It's like a disease with him—and that ridiculous playboy friend of his, Adam. You give those guys an inch and before you know it you'll be on your back and then alone.'

The interior of the Jeep stayed silent for nearly ten minutes.

'What did she say to you?'

Tara stared out through the windshield, the other woman's words echoing in her ears. She really knew absolutely nothing about Jack. It wasn't as if she'd needed the other woman to point that out to her. The thing was, everything she heard just seemed to prove the scoundrel theory. She tried to think of a more modern adage. Serial womaniser, possibly? Either way, it made him not a particularly nice guy. Certainly not the type she would ever have tried to be friends with before.

'Tara?' He reached over to squeeze her hand and got her attention. 'What did she say to annoy you this much?'

She glanced over at him, gently extricating her hand from his. 'She told me she was engaged to you.'

His jaw clenched. '*Was* being the operative word there.'

'How many fiancées have you had?'

He pursed his lips before answering. 'Dozens. That's what you expect me to say, right?'

She frowned. 'From what that woman said I really shouldn't expect much less, should I?'

'Do you believe everything everyone tells you?'

'No, I don't. But—'

'But you'd believe ill of me before you'd believe I might have my reasons—might be a half-decent guy?' He shook his head, his eyes focusing forwards. 'I actually hoped for better than that from you.'

'Look, I don't know enough about you. That's obvious. But there *were* things she said that rang true. Tell you what, then.' She folded her arms across her chest and turned to lean her shoulder against the door. 'Why don't you just explain it to me?'

'Would you believe me?' He shot her a sidelong glance. 'In the same way you believe I am who I say I am and not some imaginary character from one of your stories? Does the Jack in your story have a maniac ex-partner hanging about?'

She blinked at him. 'Well, actually….'

'Oh, that's just great. So now this is another part of the plot to seduce Tara Devlin!'

'There are coincidences between my story and all this. Even you have to admit that.'

'Some—yes.' He negotiated a turn, glancing over at her when the Jeep was straight again. 'But you can't write about relationships and not eventually mirror someone's life. Unintentionally.'

'To this extent?'

A sigh. 'My life's stranger than fiction. Nothing surprises me too much.'

There were several more minutes of silence. Then, 'Do you want to tell me about her?'

'To be honest, no.'

Tara was disappointed, despite her best intentions. It wasn't as if she'd seen anything in his personality that had suggested he was anything less than an incorrigible flirt. But some small part of her had still held a grain of hope that there was more to him than met the eye. She'd even thought, on a couple of occasions, that she'd heard a softness in his voice, seen a warmth in his eyes, that went beyond his scoundrel-like exterior.

Deep down, she'd hoped that he would need to explain things to her. Would have some plausible explanation for the accusations the woman had so readily fired in his direction. But the simple truth was, he *was* an incorrigible flirt. She'd witnessed that first-hand. Would he be able to control his flirting if he was committed to a relationship with one woman? It was only fair that he should try. Out of simple respect for that one woman if not for love of her. Tara believed in those kinds of morals. It was why she'd held out so long for a man who didn't exist beyond her imagination.

He glanced at her again. 'Do you want me to tell you about it?'

She looked out of the side window. 'It's none of my business.'

'So you're not interested, then?'

'No,' she lied outright.

He frowned. 'But I'm a villain now, aren't I?'

'I have no idea what happened between you two, and to be honest I really don't give a monkey's behind. I'm sorry if that bruises your ego.'

'You've bruised worse.' He tried to lighten the conversation. 'So, does this mean we're not spending the rest of the afternoon in bed?'

'You can spend the rest of the afternoon wherever the heck you want.' She turned to look at his profile, ignoring his attempt at brushing over the discussion. 'I intend spending it with a manuscript and my cat.'

'You're going to write something really horrible to happen to the other me, aren't you?'

'No.' She folded her arms defensively over her seatbelt. 'I actually happen to *like* the other you.'

A small smile appeared. 'What's he got that I haven't?'

A much less irritating personality, a more caring side to his nature, a higher moral standard in the way he dealt with women—the list could go on, but instead she answered with the safer, 'He's controllable.'

The statement piqued his interest. 'Is that what you look for? Controllability? Doesn't that kind of take the fun out of things?'

'I'm not looking for anything. Or anyone, for that matter. My being single and happy that way just bugs the hell out of you, doesn't it?'

He glanced away from the road again just as she turned her head to look at his profile. He noted her determined expression and swallowed a grin. 'Only if it makes you hide yourself away from the most basic of human instincts.'

'Like the need for sex?'

He looked back through the windscreen, smoothly changing gear as he spoke. 'You really have a one-track mind, Ms Devlin. Must be your profession.' His eyes twinkled as he watched her outraged face. 'I *actually* meant the need to get to know people, to build relationships with others. Do you have any family out there? Friends? People that you see more than once a month?'

She gasped, his question hitting a raw nerve. But she recovered quickly, common sense prevailing. How could he even dare to throw that at her when he was as far distant from those things as she was from being the next person on the planet Mars? He had no way of knowing or understanding anything about her life, or the things she searched so hard to find.

'I have plenty of very good friends, thank you very much, and *all* of them are a great deal nicer to be round than you.'

'Okay, then, so where do they live?'

'What?'

'Are they within walking distance, driving distance, or are they phone friends?' He hazarded another quick glance. 'Not internet friends? Could you get them any further away?'

'A friend is a friend, you moron. It doesn't matter where they live.'

'A friend is a friend if they really know you, spend time with you. Does anyone get to spend any time getting to know you, *really* know you?' He stopped at another junction, his eyes burning into hers as he waited for traffic to pass by. 'Do you let them? Because you don't make it very easy.'

Her eyes sparked at him. 'How the hell did we get onto picking my personal life to bits when we both know how very successful yours is?'

'I'm not trying to pick your life to bits. I'm trying to get to know you.' He steered across the road. 'See what I mean? You just keep on slamming the door in my face.'

'I do not! I answer your ridiculous questions.' She looked out of the side window again, muttering to her reflection. 'I knew this wouldn't work. But, oh, no, I had to go and let myself be *persuaded*.'

'You knew *what* wouldn't work?'

'What? Now you have supersonic hearing as well?' She glared at his reflection in her window.

'No, just the normal perfect kind.' He smiled at the windscreen. 'Like everything else about me.'

'Why do you have to be such a pain in the ass, Jack?'

'I'm good at it.'

'That I'll not disagree with.'

Swinging the Jeep onto the infamous Coast Road, Jack risked another glance in her direction. 'No one said getting to know each other was going to be easy. There's plenty of stuff you don't know about me—probably some things that you *really* won't like about me. Tough as I know you'll find that to believe.' He took a breath. 'But I'm sure there's just as much for me to find out about you. Hell, maybe we'll even discover things about ourselves along the way.'

Tara let his words linger in the still air of the Jeep's interior, her mind working hard. She had friends. Really she did. Okay, so she didn't see very much of some of them now that they had married and settled down. But it didn't mean she couldn't still pick up the phone and talk to them any time she wanted. And she did have a few close ones. They were always there for her, as she was for them. That was what mattered.

But the truth was she'd been alone a lot too. That was when the daydreamer had been born, happier to live in the world she created on paper than she'd often been in her own reality. There was nothing wrong with having an imagination. It had made her enough money to live her life as she wanted to. There was also nothing wrong with being content and happy while still single. No law that said she had to find some man and marry him, then diligently attempt to repopulate the planet. Tara did just fine the way she was, and Jack wasn't about to change her mind about that—or make her feel that there was something vitally important missing if she wasn't regularly sleeping with someone.

He had absolutely no right to make her question her way of life. It was downright rude. Not to mention way too early in a new 'friendship' for anyone to make such snap decisions about her. And then there was Jack's attitude to life. Because that was just perfect, wasn't it?

The Jeep pulled into the lane to their houses, bumping along the narrow tracks. When it came to a standstill by the larger of the two houses

Jack unclipped his seatbelt and turned in his seat to look at her.

'I hate the way you do that.'

Without turning she fixed him with a cool sidelong glare. 'Hate the way I do what? Breathe in and out?'

'No.' He gave a tiny smile. 'Lock me out. Your mind is turning over everything we've just said and you won't say a damn thing until you've come to some major decision about me.'

'Oh, and I suppose I should just jump in with both feet, like you do?'

'I'm not saying that.' He shook his head, bringing up one hand to brush it back through his short hair. He took a deep breath, fixing her eyes with his. 'It's just that you never give me a chance to talk it over with you. And then, if I disagree with you, we end up in some stupid debate and I have to be this wildly funny guy to keep you from stopping talking altogether.'

Tara blinked. 'And you being flippant the whole time isn't your usual demeanour?'

'I'm not an idiot, you know.' His eyes darkened. 'Just because I happen to have made a few mistakes along the way it doesn't mean I should be constantly punished for them by you and everyone else.' His words grew sharper. 'You think I'm the kind of man who sleeps with any-thing that has breasts and then leaves them with-out a thought, right? It doesn't occur to you that you don't know me well enough to make judge-ments? Or that it's unfair to take two minutes' conversation with a woman you don't know and assume I'm the reason everything went wrong?' He waited for a split second. 'I wonder just what kind of bastard do you think I am?'

Her eyes widened at his angry words. 'Don't you dare make me out to be the villain here, Jack Lewis! I'm not the one who's stood up women all over the county, having collected every single female's phone number within a week of getting here. That speaks for itself!'

Jack shook his head with a small wry smile. 'Oh, I get it. I'm some sort of—what?— *scoundrel?* Did it occur to you that as one of the very few single men aged over twenty and under ninety in a thirty-mile radius I might get some attention? Women have been forcing phone numbers into my pockets and introducing me to female family members since before I un-packed a bag. I didn't go looking for them.'

Her eyebrow raised in disbelief. 'Oh, really?'

'Yes, really.'

She stared at him until he shook his head and sighed. 'What's the point? You obviously don't believe me. But maybe if you think about it some you'll see that a scoundrel is more likely to actually *do* something with those women and then break their hearts. Instead of leaving them be and never starting anything up in the first place.'

His words twisted her heart. She watched as he shook his head yet again, shot her a sidelong glance, then turned and got out of the Jeep, slamming the door. Still sitting in the passenger seat, she took several deep breaths. The rear door opened and he began unloading the paint.

By the time he came out of the house for the second load she was leaning against the bonnet, her arms folded across her chest. 'Okay.'

He stopped on the porch and looked down at her, shoving his hands into the pockets of his jeans. 'Okay, what?'

She sighed, looking anywhere but at his face. 'Okay.' She gritted her teeth. *'You're right.'*

Jack's eyes narrowed. 'I'm right about which bit?'

He watched as her face changed, various emotions running through her eyes. She fidgeted, moving from foot to foot, then unfolding her arms to push her hands into her pockets in a similar stance to his.

'Well, about most of what you said, if that makes you happy.'

He said nothing.

'I don't know that woman well enough to judge you on what she says, and I have no right to assume you sleep with anything that has breasts just because you flirt constantly with me.'

He continued staring at her.

'And I *do* think things over carefully. I'm not used to having someone who isn't already a lifetime friend expecting me to talk them through that process. I've never had someone I don't know demand to hear my thoughts out loud. That's a pretty damned private thing, if you think about it. But I also know it's the only real way you can get to know someone else. By listening to what they think and learning about them. Rather than listening to rumours and pre-judging.'

He looked down at his feet, then back into her eyes.

Tara swallowed to moisten her dry mouth. He was making this hard. Her sensible head wanted her to tell him to get lost. Her curious mind wanted to know more about him, to find out if the tiny glimpses of warmth, the possibility of a deeper side, actually did exist. She willed him to open his mouth and tell her the story behind Sarah, to share the way he was asking her to. He had her on the local women thing—she'd have to give him that one, much as it killed her.

It did mean that she'd have to admit he might not be all bad, and that was a big step. A step she could do with some more reassurance on. But while he didn't open up about Sarah, and the story behind her, she was just going to have to take a chance and go out on a limb. The part of her soul that wanted to believe in the good side in people was determined not to simply walk away without trying to find out the truth behind the smart-ass mask he wore so well.

'If you want me to talk to you more then I'll try. But, like I said, that's a two-way street. I won't deliberately set out to judge you without knowing you a little better, but I don't think you should judge me either. I guess, in a way, I have been a touch judgemental.'

He blinked a couple of times.

She wanted to scream. It was something she wanted to do quite often when she spent more than five minutes with him.

'And, for the record, I don't think you're a bastard.'

Without the slightest change in his expression he walked down the steps and stood a few inches away from her. He continued looking down into her eyes, then raised a large hand to brush the backs of his fingers across her cheekbone. As she blinked up at him, a gentle smile appeared.

His voice was low. 'It killed you to say all that, didn't it?'

Her breath came out in a whoosh. 'Oh, yeah.'

She watched as he stepped towards her, his body not quite touching hers. She blinked again as he smiled down at her, his fingers running along her jaw and into her hair. She could see it up close this time. That hypnotising warmth of his, drawing her in. She thought moth. She thought flame. She thought sizzle. Big trouble.

His head began to lower towards her. Without thinking, she closed her eyes, her tongue automatically damping her lips. His breath fanned over her face, then his lips touched gently against her forehead.

When she opened her eyes he was grinning madly.

'Thank you.'

Torn between anger at the humiliation of not having been kissed and embarrassment at his having no doubt noticed that she had been *ready* to be kissed, Tara blushed.

'Why, you—'

'Now.' He stepped back and continued grinning. 'Don't go ruining this major breakthrough with an attack of pique.'

'You—'

'I told you.' He held his hands up in front of his body. 'I won't kiss you again until you ask me to.'

'I won't ask!'

He had the gall to wink. 'Yeah, you will. Despite your best efforts not to. You *like* me. Deep down you know you do. I challenge you.'

Tara practically growled at him.

'Admit it—you like me. Despite your best efforts not to.'

She covered her ears with her hands and started walking. 'Can't hear you—la,la,la.'

Jack laughed as she stormed away. 'And I'm *attracted* to you. Whenever you're ready to face up to that I'll be right here.'

'La, la.'

He stood by the car until he heard the slam of her front door.

He thought about Sarah for a moment, about the guilt he still carried from the mistakes of old. Truth was, he *had* been a bastard, and he knew damn well he had. He took a long deep breath at the inward confession. It had been a lifetime ago.

Then his mind turned to the present, and to Tara, and he began to smile. He was still smiling long after he'd unloaded all the paint and wallpaper.

It had been a long time since he'd had so much fun with a woman. Getting to know her was refreshing. It was a challenge. And the quick verbal banter they shared—well, it was the best foreplay he could ever remember having experienced. She was exactly what the doctor would have ordered. Smart, intriguing, sassy, sexy. A distraction of the best kind.

He didn't need to get into some heavy, serious relationship again. No way.

CHAPTER FOUR

'THIS time you've really excelled yourself.'

Jack beamed proudly upward at the peeling walls and sagging guttering. 'Yeah, she's gorgeous, isn't she?'

A dark eyebrow quirked in his general direction before green eyes looked back upwards. 'Oh, she's something, all right.'

'I fell in love.'

'Yep.' Adam Donovan nodded his head. 'Well, they do say love is blind. In your case it's apparently also brainless.'

'I'm not the one who bought a car that can do completely illegal speeds with most of the money from my inheritance.'

Adam let out a sigh as he turned to look at his latest baby. 'Yeah, but *she's* a sexual thing. *That*,' he waved his hand in the direction of the large house '—is a heap of junk.'

'You need to try looking below the surface a little more.'

They walked together up to the stairs onto the porch, Adam side-stepping to avoid a loose plank. 'Oh, I look beneath the surface.'

'I'm not talking about under a layer of clothes on one of your models.'

'Ah, now, don't go mocking what you haven't tried. You have no idea of the benefits reaped by a man from that kind of research. You're damn near a monk now.'

Jack opened the front door with a sigh. 'I am not a monk.'

'Okay, you're celibate, then.'

'I'm not celibate either.'

They stopped in front of the front door, turning to look out at the ocean. 'So you have some new love interest that I'm not aware of, then?'

Unconsciously Jack's eyes strayed to the smaller house adjacent to his. He frowned when he realised what he'd done, focusing his eyes forward again. 'No.'

Adam glanced in the direction of Jack's momentary interest. He blinked, then pursed his lips slightly. 'Neighbour?'

'Yep.'

'Male or female?'

Jack continued frowning, aware he was digging himself a large hole. 'Female.'

'Mmm.' Adam nodded, rocking back on his heels to get a better look at the smaller house. 'The right age?'

'What's that supposed to mean, exactly?'

'Not so young you could be prosecuted; not so old you'd be embarrassed to take her out in public.'

Laughter escaped, despite Jack's best efforts to stop it. 'You're a disgrace to all decent men in this country, Adam.'

'I'm needed to keep a natural balance in the world. Where would all you nice guys be without a few of us scoundrels around to make you look good?'

He had a point.

'So, what's she like?'

Jack glanced back at the whitewashed house again. 'Strange.'

'Strange in what way?'

'Your mind can just do what it wants with the word, my friend.'

Adam grinned. 'Oh, it can do a lot with that word, believe you me.'

'Centuries ago guys like you were out duelling with the decent guys most mornings at dawn.'

'Aw, c'mon—can't I show a little friendly interest?'

Jack turned and went through the large front door. 'You even *think* of getting remotely friendly with her and I may be the guy you're duelling with tomorrow morning.'

Adam followed behind. 'Don't go telling me you actually like this one? Jack, buddy, what are you trying to do here? Desert me? Who am I supposed to live the bachelor life with if you go settling down?'

'I'm not planning on getting married.'

'Ouch!' Adam shuddered as he walked down the hallway. 'You mentioned the ''M'' word.'

Opening the fridge, Jack tossed a can of soda over his shoulder before grabbing one for himself. He then turned and leaned back against the stainless steel door. 'I'm told it works for some people.'

Adam raised an eyebrow and sat on the edge of the table. Pulling the tab, he held the can away from his clothes as it fizzed, and shook his head at Jack. 'Since when did you start thinking that? I thought you'd decided that all that stuff wasn't for you.'

He shrugged. 'Never said it was.'

'Then what exactly are you saying?'

'I'm just saying for some people it works, that's all.'

'Some people like who?'

'Tess, Rachel, Lauren—they have good marriages.'

'Your sisters are women.'

'It takes two to make a marriage, pal.'

'Women like marriage better than men. It's a gender thing.'

Jack grinned. 'Is that so?'

'There is no way you're going to stand there and tell me that you haven't been better off single than tied down like you were with—' He shuddered. *'Sarah.'*

'Maybe all relationships shouldn't be judged on mine with Sarah.'

'Okay.' Adam tilted his head and managed to maintain a serious expression. 'So, using Sarah as a baseline in our little experiment here, and—I dunno—Cameron Diaz as the ideal, where exactly does the strange lady fall?'

Jack looked down at his feet for a moment, a small smile on his face when he glanced up. 'Is that with Sarah as a zero and Cameron as a ten?'

'Only a ten? Are you blind? Come on—the strange lady?'

Jack looked up at the ceiling, mentally noting the damp patch on one corner. That would need attention later. Then he took a breath. 'I'm not scoring Tara. She's…different.' He glanced across at Adam's look of disbelief, a sudden need to defend her building inside him. 'And don't bother mocking. She is. She's—hell, I don't know—interesting, challenging, *different*.'

'Oh-oh.'

'What?'

'Different is not good. Different is trouble.'

'Why can't different just be different? As in, not the kind of woman I normally meet or the kind you normally play with 'til you get bored?'

'Okay, I've heard enough.' Adam sprang to his feet and grabbed hold of Jack's shoulder, pulling him away from the fridge door before manoeuvring behind him to push him down the hall. 'You need beer and a little all-male bachelor bonding to bring you back into the real world.'

Jack smiled even as he leaned back to halt their progress out of the kitchen. 'No, I need to get on with some work on this house or I'm still going to be working on it when I turn fifty. C'mon, Adam, I've only just met this woman. It's no big deal.'

Adam stopped pushing so suddenly that Jack had to take a step back to stop from falling over. 'She's pulling you into her web. Intriguing you with her womanly ways.' He placed a hand on each of Jack's shoulders and shook him, his voice taking on a panicky edge. 'Run, Jack! Run while you still can. Don't get sucked in or before you know it you'll be wearing an apron and wheeling a pram!'

'Look, I'm not falling for her.'

Another shake. 'You said she was *different*!'

Jack placed his free hand on one of Adam's shoulders and mimicked the shaking. 'I swear to you, I am not going to marry this woman or any other woman without your express permission.'

Adam removed his hands and stood tall, nodding his head with a twinkle in his eyes. 'You better not. We're the only ones left who can stand up for the bliss that is being single. Men all over the world are relying on us. We can't let them down.'

'You know you need therapy, right?'

It had turned into a day for visitors.

'Since when do you read women's novels?'

Jack pulled the paperback out of his sister's grasp. 'Since when do you go poking through my stuff?'

Tess shrugged. 'Since always. It's part of a sister's job description. So, is there some kind of an announcement you'd like to make? Or are you just starting to realise how sad it is to still be single at your age?' She grinned. 'Maybe you're trying to pick up a few pointers?'

'That's funny.'

'I thought so.' She grabbed the book back from him, studying the cover carefully. 'I've read this. If you're going to pick up pointers then this is the woman who'll teach you what you should be doing. I bet she's some fifty-year-old grandmother who's been there and got the T-shirt.'

Jack laughed out loud. 'Not this one. She lives next door.'

'No way?'

'Yes way.' He took the book out of her hand again and set it into a cupboard beside some pasta. Closing the door, he grinned at Tess's shocked expression. 'And, trust me, she's no grandmother.'

Tess raised her mug to her mouth and sipped at the contents, studying her younger brother over the rim. 'So what's she like?'

He stared towards the window, just able to see the edge of Tara's picture window from the kitchen. 'She's different.'

'And you like her?'

Blue eyes locked with their absolute match. 'Could be.'

'You sleep with her yet?'

'Tess!' He waved a finger at her, his tone warning. 'Don't. There are limits.'

'Since when? We trained you better than that. There's no way, with four sisters, you weren't going to be taught to talk. No secrets. Remember?' She set her mug down in the sink and glanced at him from the corner of her eye. 'We all know where not talking got you last time.'

'She's not that bad.'

'You thought that about Sarah once too.'

'I learned from that mistake.'

Tess thought for a moment, then stepped closer to give her brother a hug. It still amused her that she had to stand on tiptoe to hug him. He'd been her little brother for so long that she still tended to think of him as little. 'I'm glad you came home for a while, Squirt.'

He tucked his chin in to look down at her. 'Yeah, me too, Noodle.'

Tess laughed, punching him on the shoulder as she stepped back. She raised a hand to the mass of curls on her head. The childish nickname had been a tribute to the spiral curls that many women paid a fortune for and nature had given Tess for free.

'Don't you think you've made enough money off these houses now to actually keep one?' She raised an eyebrow at him. 'Sam would love to have his Uncle Jack closer to home. He never shuts up about how much fun you are. Makes Pete feel about as interesting as a lump of coal.'

Jack laughed. 'Pete can *be* as interesting as a lump of coal.'

Tess flicked a dishtowel at him. 'You are talking about the man I love. Lay off him. Just because he doesn't do the outdoors stuff that you do it doesn't make him a bad person.'

'Oh, I'm sure he's much better at *indoor* sports.'

'Jack!' She blushed a fiery red. 'You really can be horrible.'

'Old habits die hard. But you love me really.'

She smiled affectionately. 'So, what about it? Would it be so awful living close to us again?'

With all of his sisters within a forty-mile radius, Jack had to admit it had been easy to make the decision to buy this particular house. He'd missed them. When his mother had left they'd become a tight-knit unit. Four mothers in one household. And Jack loved every one of them for it. But there was a part of him that still stung from the past: guilt, probably. It was easier to just keep moving around. No ties, nothing that he was so close to that he would mess up again. Maybe that made him chicken. But whatever worked, right?

'Well, it would be tough, I'll admit—what with you guys reproducing at the rate you are.' He smiled as he spoke. 'I mean, I don't want to be some handy full-time babysitter or anything...'

'You know you love it.'

'I'll admit I may have a soft spot or two for the tykes.'

'So stay.'

'It'll take a least a year to get this place right, so you've definitely got me for that long.' His eyes strayed to the window again. 'After that we'll just have to see.'

Tess followed his gaze. 'Should I meet this woman?'

'Who?'

Moving to stand beside him, she cocked her head to one side and studied the smaller house. 'Marilyn Monroe. You know exactly who I mean.'

Jack cleared his throat. 'I've only known her two minutes. How about I persuade her to like *me* first, then you guys can work on her?'

'Doesn't she like you already? I thought everyone did.'

He pointed at the last of the bruising on his eye. 'Does it look like it?'

'You're kidding? She *hit* you?' Tess turned his face towards her to study the damage up close. 'What the hell size is she to pack a punch like that?'

He smiled wryly. 'It's a long story.'

Tess raised an eyebrow. 'Did you deserve it?'

A broad grin answered her. 'Yeah, probably.'

'Then my sympathy levels just dropped.'

'Gee, thanks, sis.'

They smiled at each other for a few moments, then Tess nodded. 'You could do with someone in your life. Someone who'll keep your interest long enough for you to stay still for more than five minutes.'

'Hey.' He reached out to tug at a curl. 'I got the hint about staying already; you don't need to push it. And I do just fine on my own. Single life is good.'

She swatted his hand away. 'No, Squirt, you need someone. You need to try again. Have a little faith in yourself—get over the past. You're a guy, after all. You have needs like every other guy. You can't hide that from me.'

'I could never hide anything from you, and it cost me a fortune growing up.'

'And I intend continuing to collect bribe money from you for years to come.' She smiled affectionately. 'Go on, Jack. In the words of someone really wise, get a life.'

A cat came screaming through Tara's open doorway, followed by a filthy bundle of what she assumed was dog, and an even dirtier bundle of small boy. They circled her living room twice before cat and dog made an escape. The child wasn't quite so lucky.

'Whoa, there. Wait one tiny minute, kiddo.'

The child struggled in her arms, his small legs flailing. 'Lemme go!'

'I will if you promise not to run around like a loony.'

'Lemme go!'

She marched towards a stool at her breakfast bar and set him down on it, knowing that his legs wouldn't reach the floor. 'Am I at least allowed to know who it is running round my house after my poor cat?'

He blinked at her with wide blue eyes. 'Not allowed to talk to strange people.'

Tara smiled at his pouting lower lip. 'And I'm strange, am I?'

'Don't know you,' the boy huffed.

Tara mimicked him, her lower lip jutting out. 'Don't know you either.'

'Sandy will get lost.'

'Sandy?' She glanced towards the door. 'Is that your dog's name?'

'Uh-huh.'

'I'm Tara.' She held out her hand.

The boy blinked a couple of times, then scratched his head through a mop of dark curls. 'Sam.'

She smiled widely as he shook her hand with a solemn stare. 'Hello, Sam. It's nice to meet you. Are your parents down on the beach?'

'My mum's in that big house.' He pointed past her shoulder.

'Jack's house?'

A nod of dark curls.

Leaning back slightly, Tara studied the boy's features. With an almost calm resignation she recognised the resemblance to Jack. His son?

She was vaguely disappointed. Why hadn't he told her? She'd thought all men boasted about their kids—especially if one kid was a boy.

'Do they know you're over here?'

He shrugged.

'They might think you're lost if you stay away too long.'

Sam seemed to ponder that idea for a moment. Then he smiled—a killer smile in the making. Obviously a trait inherited from his father.

'Do you have juice?'

Tara couldn't help but smile back. 'I might have.'

'Can I have some?' He considered briefly. 'Please.'

Moving around the breakfast bar, Tara opened cupboard doors, locating fruit juice and a plastic beaker. 'I don't suppose you'd be interested in a biscuit?'

'What kind of biscuit?'

She smiled, adding water to his juice. 'What kind would you like?'

Again there was a moment or two as he pondered the question. Tara assumed that to be a trait of his mother, because it sure as heck wasn't inherited from Jack.

'I'd like one with chocolate on it, please.'

'Yeah, I thought you might.' She handed him the beaker, then opened a high-level cupboard to remove a container. Looking from side to side, she lowered her voice to a conspirator's whisper. 'You have to promise not to tell I have chocolate in my house, okay?'

He blinked. 'Doesn't your mummy allow you chocolate?'

'No, my *tummy* doesn't allow me chocolate.' She pushed her stomach out in front of her and patted it, blowing air out into her cheeks. 'It makes me very fat.'

Sam giggled. 'It doesn't make me very fat. I can have lots.'

'You're very lucky.'

After a loud gulp of juice followed by half a biscuit he continued, his mouth full, 'You're not very fat now. Haven't you had any chocolate today?'

Tara sat down opposite him, her chin resting on her hands. 'I can only have a little bit every now and again, when I'm good. It took me a very long time not to be fat any more. So I'd like to stay this way.'

'*You* were fat?'

Her head shot upwards at the sound of Jack's voice. He was leaning against the doorframe, a filthy dog squirming against his chest as he raised his eyebrow questioningly.

'Really?'

'Oh, yeah. Big-style.' She nodded, her eyes cool.

'How fat? Women often exaggerate that.' He held the dog away from his well-smeared T-shirt. 'Sandy, you can stop that now.'

'Beach ball with fingers fat.'

Sam's blue eyes followed the conversation back and forth, his small hand reaching out for more biscuits. 'Beach balls don't have fingers.'

'Well…' Tara smiled '…if they did, that's how I looked.'

Jack was intrigued by this new information. His eyes scanned what he could see of her above the breakfast bar, his memory filling in the rest. He drank in the sight of her with a sudden sense of hunger. Had it really only been twenty-four hours since he'd last seen her? He smiled. She sure as hell didn't look like a beach ball now. With or without fingers. In fact she looked pretty damn good to him.

Tara was what a woman should look like. His eyes wandered from the top of her honey-blonde head to her full mouth, along the smooth line of her neck to the full curve of her breasts. She was rounded in all the right places as far as he was concerned, yet still light enough for him to swing up in his arms and carry off to—

His body hardened at the vivid images his imagination supplied. He was suddenly thankful for the space in his loose sweat pants. Well, anyway, he thought she looked fine—in fact, way past fine and into the realms of gorgeous, if he was to be honest. It had been a while since he'd met a woman who wound him up without trying. Was it the challenge, maybe? The fact that she had shown virtually no interest in him in that department? Not none at all—there had been that initial response to the kiss before she'd decked him—but that wasn't enough. His ego and his libido needed more.

His eyes locked with hers. She'd witnessed his study of her body. Jack smiled, his eyes challenging her to confront him. 'You look okay now.'

Her eyebrows rose slightly. Outraged as she was by his open perusal of her in front of his son, she was still piqued by his words. '*Okay? I look okay*? Well, wow, it's been worth every pound of weight I lost to hear such a compliment.' She stood up, offering Sam another biscuit before she carefully stored away the box. 'Careful now, or you'll sweep me off my feet.'

Lord, but he'd like to. It just seemed that every step forward he took with Tara she pushed him a dozen steps back. She was different. No doubt about that. But, man, did she intrigue him.

'Is that an invitation? Because much as I'd love to oblige…' He waved the dog in Sam's direction, supporting it with both hands. 'It really isn't proper in front of the kid.'

The kid? That was how he referred to his son? Nice. Maybe he had so many *kids* that he couldn't remember all their names.

She clicked her fingers. 'Darn, and they do say timing is everything. Just not meant to be, I guess. Oh, well.' A sigh accompanied her amateur-dramatics tone. 'I must away and mend my broken heart.'

Sam had continued following the conversation, his mouth and hand covered in melted chocolate. When his dog was waved about in the air, he giggled. When Tara headed to the archway into the living area, the back of her hand across her forehead, he laughed.

Jack grinned at his amusement. 'Hey, you—your mother is looking for you, and this filthy lump of a thing.'

'Pot calling the kettle…' Tara sing-songed over her shoulder.

Jack continued, grinning, 'So maybe you better run over and get cleaned up.'

'At your house, Uncle Jack?'

Tara swung round as the boy was helped off the stool. '*Uncle* Jack?'

Twin sets of blue eyes stared at her. 'That's my Uncle Jack.' Sam pointed upwards. 'There.'

She looked up until her eyes locked with 'Uncle Jack's'. 'Oh.'

His eyes glinted at her, his grin downgraded to a smile that twitched the corners of his mouth. Handing the wriggling bundle of fur to Sam, he instructed him, 'Go and get cleaned up. I'll see you in a minute.'

He continued staring at Tara as the boy left, the dog having wriggled into an upside down position in his arms. When they were gone he folded his arms across his broad chest, the muscles in his forearms tensing.

Tara swallowed hard, her mouth suddenly quite dry. She watched as his eyes continued to glisten, then he started to walk towards her.

'You thought Sam was mine.'

She reversed in time to his steps. 'Erm, well, the thought crossed my mind. Strong family resemblance, you know…'

He kept coming. 'You think I have some hidden cache of children stowed away that I haven't mentioned, and—' He stopped for a moment, his mind working. 'And I'm guessing an equal number of mothers to go with them—right?'

Glancing frantically around her suddenly tiny living room, she improvised, 'Well, you know, it's just so easy to imagine—what with those devastating good looks of yours and that natural way you have with romance.'

His chin raised an inch, his chest puffing slightly. 'Despite the sarcasm in there I'm taking that as a compliment.' His forward journey continued. 'But, just so you know, you owe me.'

She hesitated, her eyes flicking towards his face. 'Owe you what?'

'Another apology.'

'Like hell.'

'No.' He unfolded his arms, moving ever closer. 'You *judged* me again. You just can't help yourself.'

With a quick sidestep Tara managed to place the sofa between herself and his large body. Her hands resting on its back, she leaned forward slightly. 'I will *not* apologise to you again. You bring these assumptions on yourself, really you do. It's what comes of being such an incorrigible flirt. You just can't help yourself.'

'I see.' He leaned forward a little too, his face straight and serious, his eyes searching hers. 'And I flirt with you at every possible occasion, do I?'

She flicked her tongue across her lips. 'You're doing it now.'

'Really?' His hooded eyes followed the movement of her tongue. 'Describe what I'm doing, then. Explain it to me and maybe I'll understand better where you get these assumptions from.'

Tara's pulse sped up, her blood scorching through her veins. He was turning her words into foreplay. The writer in her recognised that much. And yet she couldn't stop herself from playing the game with him.

'It's the way you look at me.'

'How do I look at you?'

She raised her chin, determined to show him she was no weakling he could seduce with a few looks and a word or two. 'You *touch* me with your eyes. Sometimes you can be so damned intense that it feels like your hands are where you're looking.'

His eyes strayed back to the swell of her breasts, the pupils growing dark as he watched their rise and fall increasing. 'Everywhere I look?'

Her traitorous body responded with a wave of warmth to her abdomen. 'You see me as some kind of challenge. You may even want me a little just because I fight you off so hard.'

Jack's heart thudded violently against the wall of his chest at the low tone of her words. He'd only read a little of her work at home, flicking through the pages to read her descriptions of intimacy between the main characters. It had turned him on. But it was because *she'd* written the words, not because of the words themselves. The fact that those images had come from *her* mind, *her* imagination, had heated him faster than in his entire life before. What she'd just said couldn't have been truer.

'You sure of that?'

Her eyes moved down across his chest, rested on the front of his sweat pants for a few seconds, then moved back up to meet his. 'I can see it.' She smiled slowly as his eyes widened. *'In your eyes.'*

He stifled a groan. 'Ask me.'

'Ask you what?'

He continued staring at her. 'Ask me to kiss you.'

She studied his face for a few moments. He really was the sexiest man she'd ever seen, outside of her imagination. And her imagination had played plenty with his physical attributes since he'd arrived next door. But up close she had even more information to play with. She now knew his eyes grew darker when he was aroused, the black pupils enlarging until they almost met the black rim that edged the blue. She could see he had long eyelashes, fanning his cheeks each time he blinked. She took her time studying him, her gaze moving up to his light brown hair with its neatly cut edges and short spiking style, then down over his eyes to his straight nose, to the slightly parted sensual curve of his mouth.

Should she ask him? Should she submit to the sheer maleness of him and allow herself that experience? It would certainly be more research than she'd ever done in her entire life. But this was a man she found it difficult to spend more than ten minutes with without arguing over the smallest thing. He irritated the hell out of her on a daily basis. So how could she be physically attracted to him?

Jack watched her study him, his breathing choppy. 'You want me to, so what's stopping you?'

A slow smile appeared. 'I'm trying to decide whether it's worth it.'

'A simple kiss?'

'Oh...' She laughed. 'I'm quite sure there wouldn't be anything simple about it. Would it end with a kiss? Can you guarantee that?'

He knew precisely where he wanted it to end, and there would certainly be kissing involved, but... 'It would end where you wanted it to. If you want it to end with just a kiss that's fine. But if you want more than that—'

'You'd oblige?'

He smiled a little crookedly. 'I'd find it hard to say no.'

'And then what?'

A deep breath. 'Sensational se—'

'After that?'

'Well, I'm fairly sure I know enough to keep us occupied for a few—'

'A few what, Jack?' She stood a little taller, her face completely straight. 'A few nights? A few afternoons, maybe? A few weeks or months? Until you sell that big old house and move on to your next fun-filled destination?'

He blinked, his voice seductively soft. 'What are you afraid of?'

It was a turn she hadn't expected. *Was* she afraid? Of what? Of him finding out she wasn't a sex goddess in bed? That she was a real person with real flaws—and the odd little touch of dreaded cellulite? Well, there was that.

But then it wasn't as if she'd had that much experience with men like Jack. Boys in college and young men in her first jobs hadn't been that interested in dating a beach ball with fingers. Yeah, she'd had a pretty face and a great per- sonality, but her defensive banter had warded off many of the few who had looked at her in the first place. None of them had been over six feet of sheer, tough-edged testosterone. None of them had looked as if they could throw her over their shoulder and carry her off to their cave for a few weeks of exhaustive pleasure.

And then there was the whole emotional thing. She wrote about *romance*, for crying out loud. Maybe it made her expectations of men in real life a little too high. But she wanted what she wrote about or nothing at all. The love, the loyalty, the soul mate. A hero of sorts. She deeply needed to believe in those things. Casual sex for the sake of it was just not Tara Devlin's style. No matter how much the man affected her. No matter how much she desperately wanted to experience passion at its most physical level, to learn what all the articles in women's magazines were really about—

'You're doing it again.'

'Doing what?' Her voice was slightly breathless.

He smiled slowly. 'Thinking, not talking.'

She smiled slightly in return. 'Yes, I am.'

'So, what is it you're thinking?'

'About what sleeping with you would be like.'

There was a sharp intake of breath. 'Really?'

She laughed nervously. 'Well, not the actual logistics of it, more the *effect* of it.'

'And?'

Her eyes glanced down to the back of the sofa, where her fingers were tugging at the edge of a throw cover. 'It's not that I don't find you a little...well, different...'

Ah, that word. 'Careful, now, don't pay me too many compliments in one go.'

A smile teased at the corner of her mouth as she glanced coyly at him from beneath her eyelashes. 'I'll try not to. But you have to see that I'm not the ''hop into bed with just anyone'' type. And after all we've only known each other—what? Nine days odd?'

'There's a time limit on being physically attracted to someone?'

'Apparently not.'

'So what are you saying?' He shrugged. 'We forget about this—' he waved his hand palm upwards, between her body and his '—and it'll just go away?'

She raised her chin. 'Can you *do* that?' Somehow she wasn't sure her ego would like it much if he could. It certainly wouldn't speak highly for her powers of attraction.

Jack studied her carefully, torn between frustration and anger. 'No, actually, I'm not sure that I can. Or that I want to.'

'Why me?'

He almost said, Why not you? But he caught himself in time. It just wasn't that way. Despite the fact that their relationship was...*different*, he knew that what he said next was important. Even now, as she waited for his answer, she seemed to be holding her breath, reserving her judgement. He took a deep, steadying lungful of air.

'Because I can't seem to stop thinking about you. What you're doing at each moment of the day. I wake up in the middle of the night and I wonder if you're awake, whether or not you'd hit me with something if I called over to see. Just so we can do this verbal sparring thing that we're so good at. You...*fascinate* me.'

Tara stared at him. He smiled, almost shyly. But that couldn't be right. This was Jack Lewis—flirt extraordinaire, Mr Confident.

'Okay, now you're scary.' He tried to tease her out of silence. 'Say something.'

She continued staring.

Jack squirmed inwardly. 'C'mon, I dare you.'

She continued studying him as she walked around the sofa.

'Yell, then—stir it up with another argument or two.'

Her eyes focused on his as she stepped closer to him, closing the distance between them with each small step. When her body almost touched his she raised her chin to study his face again. Then, her voice soft, she said, 'Why don't *you* ask *me*?'

He swallowed, his eyebrows creasing into a frown. 'Ask you what?'

'The question at hand.' Her smile was small. 'Have you forgotten already? Or is it that you're not up for having the tables turned on you?'

Air whooshed from his lungs as he exhaled. 'Babe, I'm *up* for anything you can think of.'

'There you go again. Flippant words.' There was another moment of thought. 'Are you scared of me? Scared that a woman might be prepared to play you at your own game?'

'Me?' One finger pointed at his filthy T-shirt. 'Scared?' He smiled a slow, purely sexual smile. 'Of you?' He shook his head, his voice low. 'Bring it on.'

As she opened her mouth to speak he laid his finger over her soft lips, silencing her. When she didn't move away he traced the shape of them, his rough fingertip impossibly gentle. His eyes scorched her skin with their heat, and he ran his thumb along her bottom lip. 'What was that question again?'

Swallowing to moisten her dry mouth, she smiled.

He stepped in closer, bridging the inches that separated them. His other hand moved to her hair, toying with the ends where they touched her neck. 'Yeah, I remember. It was something about a kiss.'

Tara felt her pulse beat hard in her veins as he laid the back of his hand against her throat. Her eyelids grew heavy. So this was seduction.

'You can't deny we have this. Neither of us can. I affect you as much as you affect me. Here.' He moved his hand from her neck to lift her smaller hand and place it on his chest. 'Feel.'

She watched as he held her hand against him, felt the thudding in his hard chest, fast enough to equal her own. Her stormy eyes looked back up.

The voice was husky. 'Kiss me, Jack.'

She watched as his head tilted towards her, his breath mingling with her own. This was what it felt like to really want someone. It was so much more powerful than the words she used to describe it. So much more basic than she'd been ready to admit. Her head wanted to cry out that she didn't know this man well enough to trust him with her body. Her heart wanted her to wait for more from him, a gradual build of trust and mutual respect before she could surrender herself to him. Her body simply told her mind and heart to shut the hell up and just *feel*.

When his mouth was inches from hers he waited, his eyes questioning. His breath fanned out across her cheeks, his nose touching against hers while the air crackled in the small space between their bodies.

'Well, since you ask…'

CHAPTER FIVE

THE moment their mouths met Tara knew she was in way over her head. Usually it was the build-up, the tension before the kissing, that was the most exciting part for her. But this time the kiss was simply an unspoken promise of what might come next.

Jack's arm snaked around her waist and hauled her body tight against his. Her breasts were crushed against his chest, the thud of her heart against her ribcage blending with the beat of his until there was practically no gap in beats.

He groaned into her mouth as her lips parted to allow him access to her teeth and tongue. As her hands reached upwards to frame his face, her thumbs brushing over a vague scratch of stubble on his strong chin, she felt engulfed by him—by his rock hard strength, his now familiar male scent, the determined touch of his large hands against her back and in her hair. He was practically supporting her entire weight, which was just as well, considering how sure she was that her legs currently wouldn't hold her up.

It was so unfair. A person could live their entire life and never experience this kind of passion. And then to suddenly find it in someone who in every other way was completely unsuited to them. How could that be fair?

After long minutes of heavy breathing and tangled mouths and tongues Jack finally dragged his lips from hers. He continued to massage the back of her head through her hair, his hooded eyes studying her face carefully.

Tara stared up at him, her breathing as laboured as it would have been if she'd just run a marathon.

'I knew you'd be like this.'

An uncontrollable, sex-starved maniac? Tara moistened her lips before she spoke, stalling for a few moments to compose her thoughts. 'Like what, exactly?'

His smile was slow, even sexier up close than it was from a distance of a few feet. 'Passionate, hot—all the things that you write about and then some.'

Not normally she wasn't. 'This is a chemical thing, right? It's not like you and I gel on any other level, is it?'

One eyebrow raised in question. 'You don't know that. But there's no denying this, or the fact that it promises we'll be compatible when we do...' he winked '...the horizontal mambo.'

'*When?* Not *if?*' She leaned back against the steel brace of his arm. 'You're pretty sure of yourself, aren't you?'

'You're going to deny what that kiss just said about our compatibility?'

'Sexually, no, I'm not. But I happen to think there's more to a relationship than just sex.'

'You'd be pretty poor at romance writing if you didn't, but it's one hell of a place to start from.'

'Spoken like a man, Jack. You really are the missing link, aren't you?' She struggled out of his hold. It irritated her all the more when the movement caused her breasts to brush against his chest again, setting off yet another spark in her abdomen. 'You may think that a good roll in the hay solves all problems, but the fact that you and I can't hold a full conversation without arguing over something doesn't exactly shout compatibility.'

Jack managed to stay calm. But it was an effort. 'You have to be the most exasperating female I've ever met. It just eats you up that you're attracted to me, doesn't it?'

She glared at him. 'Yes!'

'Why?'

'Because I'm not in the market for some down-and-dirty little affair.' She closed her eyes and sighed. 'No matter how great the sex might be.'

Jack waited until she'd opened her eyes again and looked across at him. His eyes had darkened with anger. 'I think I'm mature enough to deal with being simply attracted to you. When you feel you've reached the same level of maturity maybe you'll give me a call.'

He turned to leave.

Mature enough to deal with being simply attracted to you. No one had ever wanted her plainly and simply in a physical way, and been so damn open about it. Was that all this was to him? An itch that had to be scratched?

She stepped towards him, her frustration at her own physical attraction for him spilling over into anger. 'And if I slept with you, Jack? What then? We just pop on over to visit any time the need comes upon us? Once a week, maybe? How do you see this working, exactly?'

He stopped dead and swung on her. 'Why does it need to work a particular way? Why does everything need to be written in stone before it even happens?'

She gaped up at him, her eyes flashing. 'Because maybe I'm not prepared to be used as some kind of scratching post while you're here. Maybe, just maybe, I happen to think I'm worth more than that!'

'Have I ever said that you weren't?'

His sharp answer caught her off guard. Had he? Had he ever hinted that he didn't actually genuinely like her? Had he ever come out and said they should just have an affair? Truth was, he'd done neither. So what was it she wanted from him, exactly? Declarations of love and a ship to sail off into the sunset on hardly seemed like an option. Her inability to deal with an actual real-life attraction to someone was proving far more difficult than even she could have imagined. Fiction was the easier option.

Jack shook his head. 'You think I can make any more sense of what's going on here than you can?' He smiled wryly. 'It's obviously the difference between the sexes, isn't it? You want some kind of commitment from me before you'll even contemplate giving in to what you feel physically, and I'm happier with the idea of just waiting and seeing where this might go.'

Which was one hell of a step for him. The realisation knocked him back on his heels for a moment.

He blew out a puff of spent air from his lungs. 'One of us is going to have to bend on this, Tara, or we're going to have to spend the next year avoiding each other to try and forget about it. Either way, it's here. And we have to deal with it.'

With two steps he was in front of her and staring down into her face. 'I won't make a promise to you I can't keep. It's a mistake I won't make twice in one lifetime.'

He studied her eyes for a moment, before turning and marching out of the open doorway, leaving Tara behind with an open mouth and an ache in her chest that refused to shift. One of them was going to have to bend. He was right. It just damn well wasn't going to be her!

Just when she'd managed to think up a suitable retort, footsteps sounded from her kitchen. 'Oh, no, you don't. You can't make a statement like that and then just trip back in here to try and kiss and make up.'

'Much as I'd love to kiss you, I'd far rather kiss that incredible hunk of male that just left your house.'

Tara's eyes widened in shock at the sight of her friend. 'Lizzie? What are you doing here?'

Lizzie's dark eyes sparkled mischievously. 'Interrupting something good, judging by the dirt on that man's shirt and the similar smear you're wearing on yours.'

Tara looked down at the smudges of mud across her breasts. Damn him. 'Great—that's just great.'

Lizzie followed her down the hallway to her bedroom, leaning against the doorframe as Tara pulled the shirt off and threw it in the linen basket. 'You did remember it's a pre-hen night weekend, right? Because if you've got one of him for each of us I swear I'll do your laundry for ever.'

Tara yanked open a dresser drawer with more force than necessary, pulling it completely out and depositing all the contents on the floor. Swearing loudly, she set the empty drawer on the end of her bed and tugged a bright T-shirt over her head before throwing things in the drawer's general direction.

Lizzie sniffed. 'Do I smell sexual tension in the air?'

'There's sexual tension in Tara's house?' An elegantly dressed figure appeared by Lizzie's side, helping to completely block the doorway. 'And it's not on paper? I find that tough to believe.'

'I know—who'd have thought it? But I've always reckoned all that information had to come from somewhere, so maybe Mr Studly is research.'

'Hell, *I'd* research him—all night long and into the wee small hours.'

Tara glared at her friends. 'He'd probably enjoy that.'

Two sets of eyes studied her intently from the doorway as she pushed the drawer back into its allotted slot. She glanced across at them as she smoothed her hair down with her hands. 'What?'

Lizzie shrugged. 'Nothing at all. Nope—nothing on my mind.' She turned to the taller woman. 'You, Laura?'

Laura shook her head. 'Can't think of anything offhand.'

'No, nothing new with us.'

Tara threw her hands up in exasperation. 'Okay, okay. You want to know who he is then just ask me. It doesn't have to be the Spanish Inquisition.'

Immediately the two women landed on the soft bed beside her, their smiles infectious as they spoke in unison.

'So, who is he?'

'How long have you known him?'

'Have you slept with him yet?'

'Has he a brother?'

'Stop!' Tara yelled at the top of her voice, before laughing with them. 'If you two are going to ask me ten million questions then we need wine.'

They followed her to the kitchen, their voices animated. 'Lots of wine—and munchies, if this is a long story.'

Laura smiled at Tara's back. 'God, I can't remember the last time you slept with someone. What was it? Around about the early nineties?'

'That's funny.'

'Tara had *sex*?'

Tara rested her head against the heavy wood of the breakfast bar, her words aimed at the ground as the third member of the party arrived. 'Next year I'm spending the summer writing in Outer Mongolia so no one can visit me.'

Mags kissed the top of her head. 'Sweetie, we'd find a way of having a party there too. Traditions are a darlin' of a thing.'

Tara squinted upwards and to the side. 'Don't we have an official hen night for Lizzie in a couple of weeks? We could make this a less frequent tradition, you know.'

A wine glass was placed into her hand, beside her head, and a voice sounded beside it. 'You weren't complaining when everyone picked on me after I dumped Donald.'

There was a ripple of laughter from the assembled crowd. 'Yeah, but that was funny. After dating Mickey you only have to find a Pluto and you'll have had a complete set!'

Tara's shoulders shook. 'You guys are truly evil.' A fingernail poked her between the shoulderblades. She raised her head, glanced round at her friends, then downed half her glass's contents. 'His name is Jack.'

Her glass was miraculously refilled, the bottle then making a round of the kitchen as tall stools were dragged up to the breakfast bar. 'And he lives next door.'

'He didn't live next door last year.'

'No, we'd have noticed.'

'Hell, we'd have baked.'

Tara was surrounded by a hug from a smaller version of Lizzie. 'He's married, isn't he?'

Grey eyes met brown. 'What made you think that?'

'I saw his wife and kid leaving as we drove in.'

'Mags, that was his sister and her boy.'

Mags hugged her again. 'Thank God for that.' She leaned back to grin and wiggle her eyebrows. 'Hubba-hubba.'

Laughter spread around the room again.

Jack had bumped into the first two of the gorgeous women brigade on his way out of Tara's house. The idea had crossed his mind that maybe Tara had some kind of emergency alarm that sounded when she was kissed, alerting the cavalry to come to her rescue. The thought had amused him.

He was in much better humour after a cool shower and something to eat. In fact, he even persuaded himself he could feel a little smug. After all, *he* was mature enough to deal with this fierce attraction he had for her. It wasn't *his* fault she was incapable of dealing with pure physical attraction. Even if it was the strongest physical attraction he'd ever encountered himself.

After Tess and Sam had left he'd more time to think. He had a feeling Tara's experience of physical attraction was probably less extensive than his own. Not that he kept a bedpost for notches… But Tara seemed to live this reclusive lifestyle of her own choosing. As if women didn't have the same basic needs and desires as men!

He was just sick to death of women who wanted to put a noose round his neck. That wasn't his way. If he'd wanted to be settled so badly then he'd have just married Sarah—maybe even had a couple of kids by now. But he'd known in his gut it wasn't for him.

Jack wanted the freedom to choose. To make his own decisions. Was that so much to ask for?

If Tara was the least bit interested in what he was like she would try actually getting to know him before she made up her mind that he was some womanising waster. Because he wasn't that either. He was just a guy who wanted to live his life, earn a reasonable living, have pride in himself and what he did. Was that a crime? Surely if she took the time to really know him then maybe she would just give it a try. They could go with the flow, see where the road took them. That kind of thing.

If she couldn't do that—let go for a while—then why should he be the only one taking a chance? After all, what if she was *needy*? If he was looking for needy he could have dated any of those local women who had been so desperate to pin him down when he'd first arrived. It had been like being the prize in a contest, for crying out loud.

Nah. The last thing he needed was another female watching his every move and accusing him of things he hadn't done, picking away at their relationship until it lay in ruins because she didn't trust him. Not again. Been there—got the T-shirt.

With a beer in his hand, he sat down on the porch to watch the sun disappear into the ocean below. Laughter drifted across from Tara's house as he allowed the cold liquid to slide down his throat.

'Hi, there.'

He uncrossed his long legs and turned to look at the small woman standing beside him. 'Hi—and you are…?'

'I'm Mags.' She stretched a hand towards him. 'A friend of Tara's from the city. And you're Jack, right?'

Jack shook her hand, his eyebrow rising slightly. 'Did she send you over?'

'Hell, no. She'll flip when she knows what I'm doing.'

'And what exactly *are* you doing?'

Mags grinned, dimples appearing in her cheeks. 'It's my sister's wedding in a couple of weeks, so we're here for a girls' night out. Some of us thought it might be a good idea to let you know where we're going.'

'In case the police come looking for you?'

'No. Though it wouldn't be the first time if that happened.'

Jack blinked. 'Okay.'

'It's just, if you know where we're going then you might maybe want to stop by for a drink later on—you know, as a surprise thing.'

'Oh, it'd be a surprise.'

She stepped forward, her voice low as she leaned towards him. 'Tara doesn't always make it easy for guys to get close to her.'

That raised a smile. 'You think?'

'Oh, I *know*. I could give you a list as long as your arm.' Her eyes studied his muscled limbs. 'Well, maybe not *your* arm, exactly, but a pretty long list anyway—of guys she's blown off who would have been great for her.'

'And how do you know *I'd* be great for her?'

Her eyes sparkled. 'Jack, anyone who has her this irritated inside such a short amount of time can only be good for her. It's about time she had a shake up in her life. And you look like the kind of guy who would shake her properly, if you get my drift.'

He stared at the woman for several silent moments. 'And if I decided I wanted more than just some shaking up in *my* life?'

Where in hell had that come from?

'Then, honey, you'd need all the help you could get.'

He reached his hand out again. 'It's nice to meet you.'

She accepted his hand again with a mesmerised smile. 'Pleasure's all mine, Jack. Oh, and Laura said to ask if you had any brothers?'

The bar was packed solid. Wall-to-wall human beings, and some whose origins were somewhat in doubt. And Jack was caught in the middle of it all, watching Tara and her friends with great amusement.

It hadn't taken long to find the women in this small country bar. They stood out like the proverbial sore thumbs. Something to do with being quite loud and more than a touch crazy. That and the fact that they were attracting the attention of every male in the room under the age of ninety.

They were all dressed innocently enough—no ridiculously short skirts or tops cut down to the navel—but they still managed to look incredible. Jack had almost choked on his soft drink when he'd first seen Tara. She really should have worn government health warnings on her back.

Just a pair of black jeans and a cropped halter neck which exposed glorious inches of her back. But it was the way she looked. Her tanned skin glowed everywhere it showed, from shoulders to wrists, from the flat stomach exposed above the waistband of her jeans to the broad expanse of her back. Then there was her neck, and the rounded breasts beneath the generously cut V of her top's neckline.

Her hair was like something from a shampoo ad—smooth and sleek, moving in a soft curtain as she turned her head. And as for her face— how did women *do* that? They somehow applied make-up to the barest minimum and yet still managed to make their eyes look huge, their lashes look twice their normal length and their lips look as if they'd just been thoroughly kissed.

Somehow she had managed to make herself look like someone who desperately wanted to be made love to, and yet he knew for a fact that she had no intention of letting him do that. Was it some kind of ancient game?

Then she walked onto the dance floor and began to move. Jack practically spontaneously combusted at the bar. That behaviour was definitely going to get her arrested. He ordered a beer and set his soft drink down.

'Is he still there?'

Lizzie danced in a circle to see, her hips swaying back and forward to the music as she looked at the bar. 'He looks like he's about to explode.'

'I hope he leaves a hole in the roof on his way out.'

'He doesn't look all bad to me.'

'That's not exactly how *I'd* have described him.'

Mags laughed as Laura shimmied down to the floor and back up. 'Yeah, well, you can put that smutty mind of yours back in its box. I think he looks nice enough, and sure as hell like he's got the hots for you, Tara.'

Tara resisted the temptation to look his way. 'Me and every other woman who doesn't look like they've just been run over by a bus.'

'Well, in all fairness I've seen at least three women drape themselves across the bar beside him, and he hasn't done anything more than smile politely at them before he's looked back at you.'

She frowned. 'Really?' She looked across at Jack as he was handed a bottle of beer. 'Three of them? Were they under the age of fifty?'

'Well under. Though the last one looked like that might have been her bra size.' Mags leaned in closer. 'Why don't you just go over there and speak to him for a while? Would that be so bad?'

Laura smiled. 'I'll go if you like.'

Tara glared at her friend. 'No, you won't.'

'But if you're not interested…?'

'I didn't say I wasn't interested. I just happen to be not very happy about it.' She left the tiny dance floor with the rest of them and sat down at their table. 'I just don't like him that much, so I find it hard to understand how I can be so attracted to him.'

'You should sleep with him.'

Mags glared at Laura. 'That gem of advice from the queen of lasting relationships.'

'If she slept with him then at least she'd know whether or not that part worked before she wasted time on everything else.'

Everyone scowled in Laura's direction.

'What?' She raised her eyebrows. 'What's the point in using the kiss and make up thing after a row if the kissing and making up isn't good?'

Lizzie was the first to break the silence. 'You're a man trapped in a woman's body, aren't you?'

Mags dabbed at her chin with a tissue after almost choking on her drink. 'Laura, you're priceless. It's just as well we all know you believe in the hearts and flowers stuff as much as the rest of us.'

'I never said I didn't. But you have to admit that kind of thing is thin on the ground now. Doctor Zhivago-type guys have long since frozen their asses off waiting to be discovered by career girls. I just think that a little jiggery-pokery goes a long way these days, when you even everything out.' Laura sighed dramatically as she came to the end of her speech. 'Not all of us put the lifelong friendship thing first like Tara does.'

'It matters.'

'I didn't say it didn't. I'm just saying I'll be equally happy with someone who can satisfy a need or two elsewhere.'

Tara shook her head. 'I'd rather put a little more emphasis on something that lasts.'

'Sex-based relationships last when the sex is good.'

Mags laughed again. 'When you've been married and had kids you'll soon realise they don't really. It takes way more than that.'

'Then you're not doing it right.'

'Oh, sweetie, we do it right. We've done it right on at least three occasions—I have the living proof.' She winked at Tara. 'Truth is, when you have three screaming kids you're just as happy with someone who can hold you as you fall asleep, or take the kids off for an afternoon to give you peace, as you'd be with someone who regularly has you hanging from the ceiling by your fingernails.'

'Not that we're underrating the value of that experience either.' Lizzie grinned over the rim of her glass.

Tara listened to the conversation for a moment while her eyes strayed back to Jack. Their eyes locked across the room and she glanced away. 'I can't help how I feel. I just need more from a guy than great sex.'

'Have you ever actually *had* great sex?'

'Laura!'

Laura glared at Lizzie. 'Well, I don't think she has, and that's why I think it would be good for her to have an affair with this guy. That way she'll know, and she'll be stronger in her beliefs one way or another because she has all the facts.'

In a weird way it made sense. But it also went against everything that Tara had always wanted from a relationship. Did she set her standards too high? Was that her problem?

'Is this guy definitely not keeper material?' Mags's hand rested over hers on the table, her eyes questioning.

'Jack Lewis?' Tara almost laughed, instead managing a graceful snort of derision. 'From what I've seen so far he has the depth of a small puddle. He's Neanderthal man—the old-fashioned strong male that we all thought didn't exist any more. I think that's part of the reason I'm so damn attracted to him.'

Mags shrugged. 'Maybe if you got to know him a little better you might discover he has some old-fashioned values to go with the rest of the stuff. Can you honestly say you've taken the time to find out?'

Tara blinked. 'No, I can't.'

'That's not like you, is it?'

'No, but I haven't been much like myself recently.'

Mags watched as her friend's eyes strayed back to the bar. She gave a small smile. 'Why don't you try asking him out?'

Grey eyes moved back to her face. 'As in a date?'

'Yeah, why not? What's the worst that can happen? You either find out you're right or you win the big prize by discovering you're wrong.'

Laura leaned forward to hiss, 'And either way you still have the opportunity for some great sex!'

'I was wondering if you'd like to dance?'

Jack stared straight ahead as she reached his side, casually bringing the bottle to his lips. 'With you?'

'I have three friends if you'd prefer someone else. Though I should probably let you know Mags is married and Lizzie is spoken for.'

She frowned at his profile.

He glanced down at the bottle in his hands for a second, then back in front of him again. 'I don't want to dance with any of your friends.'

'Don't tell me. You macho types don't dance, right?'

'You think with four sisters I never learnt to dance? Every time one of them was stuck for a date at a formal or on New Year's I got dragged along as the substitute. I could dance you under the table.'

She watched as he calmly lifted the bottle to his mouth again. 'So dance with me, then.'

He seemed to think for a moment, his lips pursed. 'Last time you asked me to do something with you it ended in disagreement.'

'Nothing unusual there.'

'I guess not.'

Taking a deep breath, and relying slightly on previously consumed Dutch courage, Tara reached out and used her hand to turn his chin towards her. 'I'm *trying* to be nice here.'

His eyes studied her cautiously. 'I thought there was something different.' He smiled slowly when her eyes widened, and he caught her hand in his when she removed it from his chin. 'Are you being nice to me because your friends told you to?'

She looked down at their joined hands. 'They may have suggested it, but I think you know only too well I don't do anything I don't want to.'

'That I do.'

He studied her bowed head for a moment, before setting the bottle behind him and standing to tower above her. He tugged gently at her hand. 'Well, come on, then. Let's give them something to look at.'

With her hand still in his, he held the other to the small of her back and guided them effortlessly through the crowd. Once on the dance floor he linked his fingers with hers and held their hands above her head to spin her round. He grinned widely when she was facing him again, pulling her against him to fit her body along the length of his.

'Now we get to find out whether or not we have any kind of natural rhythm together.'

As the beat of the fast country and western tune matched the pulsing of blood in her veins, Jack began to move her body in time with his.

She was vaguely aware of the words of the song as he guided her movements, waited until she matched his tempo, then swung her out and back into his arms. The other dancers began to clear a path for them as they built up speed. The song's bass line beat a heavy rhythm.

He spun them round in an ever-widening circle, rocking her body first from side to side, then forwards and backwards, while their hips moved together all the time. Tara started to smile as the dance floor got larger.

The chorus sounded out loud, then the singer sang it again. Their feet moved faster and faster as Jack spun them in smaller and smaller circles, the rocking continuing all the while. Even as she started to laugh with him she could see her friends standing on their chairs to get a better view.

The beat grew faster, faster still. Just when she thought the crescendo couldn't grow any more he set her away from him, their hands back above her head, and he spun her again and again until the music came to an end and he hauled her, breathless, back into his arms. The crowd broke into rapturous applause. She recognised her friends' voices in the cheers.

Jack grinned down at her flushed face. 'I'd say we have rhythm.'

'You're crazy.'

He shrugged. 'Yeah, but I can sure as hell dance.'

They laughed, and then to even more applause Jack dipped his head and kissed her.

Oh, what the hell. Tara joined in. She slipped her hands from his grasp, wrapped her arms around his neck, pushed herself up onto her tiptoes and kissed him right back. Music started up again as Jack put his arms tight around her waist and lifted her off the ground, swaying them to the music as they kissed. Tara smiled against his mouth. She lifted her head back until the ends of their noses touched.

'Okay, so you can dance. That puts you further up the evolutionary chain than the caveman.'

'Yet another thing you've managed to learn about me. That makes about two now, doesn't it?'

Once more she found herself getting lost in the blue of his eyes. 'Then I guess we're actually making some kind of progress, aren't we?'

'Well, you are.'

'And you think you're not?'

He continued swaying her in time to the music, her feet swinging inches above the floor. 'I don't think you want me to get to know you.'

Her eyebrows raised slightly. 'Why would you think that?'

'Oh, I don't know. Maybe the fact that every time we get close like this—' he squeezed his arms tighter for a second '—you start an argument over something dumb and we're back to step one again.'

'*I* start an argument?' She frowned at him for a few seconds, then calmly retorted, 'It's not always my fault. You help out.'

His smile grew at the sight of the small pout on her lips.

'Maybe I do. Maybe I don't. And maybe it's easier for you to argue with me than it is for you to try me out.'

Tara smiled. 'Like a pair of shoes?'

A shrug. 'Maybe.'

'Okay, smart-ass, I'll *try you out*. But we'll do it my way.'

'Which is what, exactly?'

'We'll go on a date and we'll try to start over. You can ask me first-date questions and I'll ask you first-date questions and we'll see if we're compatible.'

'I thought we'd pretty much established that part.'

She tried to ignore the painfully slow way he lowered her body along his before he set her feet back on the ground. 'Not that kind of compatible. The other kind. The kind where we see if we can actually learn to like each other.'

Jack took a deep breath as he stepped back from her, putting a distance between them again. She was moving them onto relationship territory—a dangerous place for any self-respecting bachelor. He looked at her, studied her face for a long moment. Hell, he was a brave guy. What was the worst that could happen?

'No strings?'

'No strings. An experiment, if you like.'

'Okay, I'll play.'

CHAPTER SIX

DINNER was Mags's idea—a stroke of genius, she felt. Tara was taking a tad more convincing.

'Try being nice to him for a change. Give the man a chance.'

'I *am* nice,' Tara huffed over the phone line. 'I'm always bloody well nice. I'm a genuinely nice person.'

'Obviously you are. You're just a bit defensive, that's all.'

Silence invaded the air for a long second. *'Defensive?'*

'Yeah, as in ''get the hell away from me, you plague-carrying vermin'' defensive. Nothing major.'

'I am *not* defensive. He's just a pain in the ass most of the time.'

'And the first man to have you this riled since the time you saw that kid trying to drop-kick a kitten.'

'I wanted to drop-kick the kid!'

'Admit it, Tara, honey.' Mags turned on her soothing 'mummy' voice. 'This man has you hot under the collar and you don't know what to do about it. He's the first one to ever come close to that ideal of yours. Sexually speaking.'

'What ideal? I don't have an ideal.'

'Yeah, you do.'

'No, I don't.'

'Yes, you *do*.' Mags sighed. 'Honey, you describe him in every book you write. Your ideal, your *hero*. He's the guy you've never managed to find in real life, so you've stayed single and shut out all the guys who didn't come close to that ideal man.'

'Because he doesn't exist outside of my imagination.'

'Outside of your fantasies, you mean.'

'Same thing.'

Mags took a breath and jumped in. 'Until this guy.'

'Jack Lewis is *not* my ideal guy.' Well, not the real one anyway.

'He's as close as you've ever come to meeting him. And I think that scares the hell out of you.'

Silence.

'You still there?'

Tara's voice was low. 'Uh-huh.'

'You okay?'

'I'm not falling for this guy, Mags. I mean it. He may be in the dictionary under "alpha male", but that's as close as he gets to being one of my heroes. Not once has one of my guys irritated a heroine into submission.'

'You like his wit. His charm. He challenges you mentally, and that's something really new for you. And he doesn't look like someone just smacked him in the face with a wet fish either, which helps.'

The statement raised a small burst of laughter. 'Gee, and I'm the one writing romance? You're wasted, you know.'

Mags smiled at her end of the line, the smile coming across in the lilt of her voice. 'Admit it, honey. You're attracted to this guy. Hell, your granny would be. You just weren't prepared for that and it's knocked you slightly off-base, that's all. Try being nice—get to know him before you dismiss him altogether. What's the worst that could happen?'

'How many disaster movies have you seen that use that exact line?'

'What are you doing in my kitchen?'

Tara glanced over her shoulder to find Jack leaning against the doorframe. 'I yelled, but you can't have heard me over all that testosterone-fuelled power tool stuff.'

He glanced down his hallway, then back to where she was unloading shopping onto one of his brand-new counter tops. 'I'll try again. What are you doing in my kitchen, Miss Devlin?'

Turning slowly, she leaned against the counter. She crossed her arms over her chest, tilted her head to one side and smiled. *Be nice.* She was going to be nice to him if it killed her in the process. Her voice came out like melted honey. 'What's wrong? Are you not pleased to see me?'

'I didn't say that.' He nodded towards the counter. 'What's the food for? You worried I might waste away?'

The smile grew as her eyes moved slowly across the dust-covered denim of his shirt and jeans and then back up. Her body warmed a degree or two. *Yum.* Definitely not a wet fish in the face kind of guy. There was a lot to be said for a well-put-together guy in work clothes. Maybe the fact that they were immediately attached to the word 'dirty'…

'Nope, not the least bit worried about that. We have a date, remember?'

Jack blinked, as much at her open perusal as at anything she was saying. 'You're going to cook for me?'

'Yes.' She shrugged. 'You sounded busy over here, so I thought I'd make it easy for you.'
Nice.

She hadn't made it easy for him since he'd arrived. He was suspicious. What was she at? Maybe she was going to poison him.

'Can you cook?'

'You'll know the answer to that in about half an hour.'

'You could have just invited me over to your place...'

That thought had crossed her mind. But this way she was in control—or so she had reasoned to herself. She could walk out any time she wanted to. Then he wouldn't think there was more than food on the menu.

'Why are you so suspicious of me all of a sudden?' She tilted her head and smiled—nicely.

Because she was a *female* cooking in his *kitchen*. It was a territory thing. When a woman cooked in a man's kitchen it was—well, domesticated. Next she'd have him in slippers, reading the Sunday papers and looking at flowery wallpaper.

'We could have gone out.'

Tara shrugged. 'You're busy. I just thought this would be easier.' Thoughtful was nice.

Now she was using common sense on him. He should start running down the hall and not stop to look back. She could keep the house.

Instead he found his voice answering weakly, 'I'll need to have a shower.'

'I can wait.'

'We could still go out, you know. I can stretch to the expense of a date.' He was groping for an escape clause, a 'get out of jail free' card. 'I'm not quite destitute yet.'

She smiled, her eyes teasing. 'You bought this place—give it time, you'll get well past destitute. Take the free meal while you can get it.'

He blinked.

Oops. She'd nearly slipped up on the 'nice' thing again. It was tough.

Taking a breath, she smiled again—a nice, *nice* smile, from the land of all things nice—and raised an eyebrow, waiting for the wheels to turn in his head.

He sighed. 'I'll have a shower, then.' A long finger waved at her. 'But you're up to something, and don't think I don't know it.'

The smile quirked slightly at the edges of her mouth. 'Well, if you know then you're safe—aren't you?'

Jack frowned at her for several long seconds, then turned and left the room. All the way up the hall he felt suddenly threatened.

It was like stepping into a big minefield. Tara was being nice to him. It was offputting.

Tara stared at him across the table. If she hadn't known he belonged in a shaving commercial before, then she sure as heck knew now.

He was downright, out and out, drop-dead gorgeous. She sipped at a glass of wine as her eyes roved over him. As Mags the Wise had once said: hubba-hubba.

Eventually he glanced up. 'Have I still got dirt on me?'

'What?'

'You're staring.' He raised an eyebrow. 'I wondered if I still had dirt on me?'

'No, not that I can see.' And she'd looked.

A slow smile began at the edges of his mouth, moving up to become a spark in his blue eyes. 'So what, then?'

She lowered her long lashes, pursing her lips for a moment as she thought. 'You just look… okay cleaned up. That's all.'

'Is that a compliment? I'll have to write the date and time down.'

Tara moved her glass about in front of her as her eyes searched the air for words. 'I've paid you compliments before, in a…*roundabout* way.'

'Nowadays most men don't see ''Neanderthal'' as a compliment.'

Clearing her throat, she glanced at him. 'They might if it's a character trait they're aiming for.'

'Old-fashioned doesn't necessarily translate as Neanderthal.'

She leaned forward slightly, matching his low tone. 'And you see yourself as old-fashioned, do you?'

'There's nothing wrong with a man believing that a woman—'

She forgot the 'nice' theme for a moment. 'I swear, if you say ''should know her place'' you'll be wearing red wine as part of that little ensemble you have on.'

He grinned. 'Actually, I was *going* to say that a woman should be able to lean on him every now and again. Let him take some of the load off her. There's nothing wrong with that, I assume?'

She grinned at him. 'Well-rescued.'

Laughing, a low rumble from deep in his chest, he leaned back in his seat. 'You really carry the feminism banner high, don't you?'

Tara waggled a finger at him. 'That's definitely an argument waiting to happen. Breadsticks at dawn.' She smiled. 'Anyway, I'm a little old-fashioned myself. I have to be, writing historical fiction for a living. It's in the job description.'

'So you're a modern-day woman with old-fashioned values? How does that work, exactly?'

'Don't make fun of me.'

'I wasn't.' His gaze was steady. 'This is what we're supposed to be doing here, isn't it? Asking questions and getting to know each other? That was the whole idea behind a date, right?'

She studied him cautiously. He'd returned from his shower less suspicious and unusually smiley. He was up to something and it worried her. Maybe she'd been too nice and it had made him think he was onto a sure thing?

She gave him the benefit of the doubt, and realisation entered her brain with the speed of a hundred-year-old turtle. 'You're not comfortable with this, are you?'

'Me?' He avoided her direct gaze. 'Nah, I have women cook in my kitchen all the time.'

She merely raised an eyebrow and sipped at her wine.

A second or two passed before he let his breath out in a huff. 'All right, I'll confess I'm not too comfortable in the land of domestication.'

'You should have said something.'

His eyes searched for hers. 'So, another tick on the ''Things that make Jack unsuitable'' list? You think because I'm not completely comfortable with you cooking and taking over my kitchen it makes me some kind of weirdo, right?'

'I didn't say that.'

'Has anyone ever told you you're judgemental?'

Nice left the room—at speed. 'I am not judgemental!'

'You see me as some guy who thinks women only belong in the bedroom, preferably in their own house and not mine, so I can sneak off home before sunrise?'

'Now who's being judgemental?' Even if he *was* walking down the right road...

They stared at each other across the battle-field. Tara steamed inwardly at his accusation, as much annoyed by the fact that he was so close to the mark as she was by the fact that she'd only two minutes ago foregone being judgemental and given him the benefit of the damn doubt. He really was very ungrateful.

But she did keep on placing him into the 'caveman' box. That was true. Maybe by choosing to think of him that way she was protecting herself from actually finding out what was beneath the surface. Or from being disappointed by what she found there. It was a safety thing. She had already made the other Jack Lewis into an alpha male with a caring and warm interior. *Her* Jack was real to her, different from the Jack who sat in front of her, the person she perceived this Jack to be. If she found out the real Jack had that interior too, she would be in big, big trouble.

Because she was already halfway in love with the one she'd created. The one she'd based on the reality outside her window.

Her eyes widened slightly at this shocking revelation.

'Okay, so what's the conclusion you've drawn now?'

She glanced around the room, avoiding his eyes, and back-pedalled as best she could. 'Who says I've come to any conclusion?'

'You had that frown between your eyes again, which normally indicates you've been making some major decision. So what is it?'

Tara panicked and came up with the first excuse she could think of. 'It's your size.'

He blinked. 'I beg your pardon?'

'I think I'm a little intimidated by your size.' She blushed, realising the hole she'd just jumped into. 'Maybe that's why I keep thinking of you in caveman terms. It's not because I think you have low morals or no heart.'

Jack digested the revelation carefully. 'So because I'm taller than you—'

'And broader.' The words rushed out on their own. She set her wine glass a little further away from her. That was quite enough of that stuff!

'Okay, because I'm *larger* than you, you feel—what? Intimidated? So you get all defensive on me?'

Tara cleared her throat quietly. 'It's not just your size. It's the way you fill up a room when you're in it. Maybe it's the fact that if you really wanted to you could make me do something when I didn't want to, just because you're stronger than me.'

'And you think that's the kind of man I am?'

'No!' Her eyes locked with his. That had come out wrong too. Someone should just shoot her. 'No, I don't think that.' She saw the disbelief in the blue depths. 'Really. It's just the very fact that you could. That's why dinner here's safer, you see…'

An eyebrow raised in question.

Her heart thudded against her ribs. 'This way I can leave if I feel threatened by the way you make me feel sometimes.'

He continued to stare at her.

'Well, you need to see it from my point of view.' If she'd had a gun she'd have shot herself. 'The whole size thing is intimidating because—well…' She reached for the wine glass again, her mouth dry. 'I guess it makes me feel very small and a little bit…feminine. In a fairly basic sense.' She took a deep breath, closed her eyes, and let the words spill out in a sprint. 'And I've never really experienced that before.'

Well, that was great. If he hadn't been uncomfortable before, he sure as hell was now. Jack blinked and forced himself to think calming thoughts. After all, it wasn't as if he was some hormonal teenager. Or he hadn't been until a couple of weeks back. He just needed a second.

He nodded slowly, his eyes looking everywhere but at Tara.

'Okay.'

It was Tara's turn to stare. 'That's all you're going to say?'

He pushed some salad around with a fork, his head bowed. 'What else do you want me to say?'

'I don't know—maybe that you understand a little better where I'm coming from. Anything at all like that.' She frowned at him. 'You're not going to tell me that knowing that fact has no effect on you?'

'No-o, I'm not going to say that.' He glanced up. 'You just don't want to know the effect it has on me right now.'

She blushed an even fierier red as his meaning sank in. 'It just keeps coming back to sex with us, doesn't it?'

'I think we've established the fact that the chemistry is there, yes.'

They picked through the food on their plates for a few moments before Jack spoke again. 'I guess I'm just as much thrown on my ear by all this as you are. I saw you being here, in my kitchen, as some kind of a threat.'

'Where would you rather have gone?'

He smiled sheepishly. 'I'd probably have picked a meal in the bar on the other side of the bay. The place has a great open view down across the ocean, big comfy chairs and a relaxed atmosphere. And I wouldn't have had to wear a tie.'

Tara smiled at the thought of him in a tie. 'It's just a little old tie. It's not like you wear one every day.'

A grin appeared as they headed for safer ground. 'I used to have to wear one every day, so I guess that's where the aversion comes from. Somewhere in my mind it probably symbolises how trapped I felt at the time.'

The words piqued her interest. 'You had an office job?'

Somehow she couldn't picture him behind a desk. It would have had to be a really big desk. Otherwise he'd have looked like a grown-up sitting at one of those primary school desks—like Alice after the 'drink me' potion.

A quick nod, then he chewed some food before answering. 'I was an architect.' He glanced up again. 'Still am—technically. I just got to realise I wanted to do the work myself rather than watching other people do it.'

'Really?' The word sounded more disbelieving than she had intended. Not nice at all. 'Sorry, that came out badly.'

He smiled, his eyes twinkling. 'Smashed a preconception, did I?'

'Possibly, yes. Don't you miss the security, though? Surely it paid better?'

The corners of his mouth twitched. 'I do okay. As well as the places I work on I'm a partner with another guy—Adam—in a small company building houses to order. I do the designing—one-off specialist stuff that people request—Adam looks after the business end. I really hate that stuff.' A shrug. 'We're pretty much booked solid.'

Tara blinked. 'That's nice.'

Jack laughed aloud. 'Okay, then, now you know my sordid secrets, what about you? You always been a writer?'

She shook her head. 'No, but I was always a daydreamer. I sent stuff off for years before I finally sold something, but I do okay now, and my parents provided well enough for me to have a cushion so I don't have to worry if a commission cheque is late. Guilt money, you know…'

He caught the wistful tone in her voice, noted the sudden sadness in her eyes and knew instinctively. 'They're gone?'

'Yeah, a few years now.' She shrugged. 'They were both fairly career-orientated, and eventually they didn't have time for each other. Usual story: divorce, guilt over the kids, competing for our love, that kind of thing. Nothing out of the ordinary.'

Jack leaned forward again, setting his elbows on the edge of the table. 'Is that why you're still single?'

'Oh, yeah, that's the reason all right. I have to beat men away from my door every day. You didn't see the queue earlier?'

'Must have slipped my attention.'

'Ah.' Twisting her tall glass between her fingers, she smiled across at him. 'You need to be more observant of these things.'

Jack sat back. He studied Tara's face, trying to read between the lines of her words. It wasn't easy, but it was rapidly becoming a necessity.

'So how come *you're* still single, then?'

'Luck?' He grinned.

Tara ignored that. 'You're the youngest in your family?'

'Yep, the baby.' He continued grinning, despite having had the conversation turned on him. 'And was alternately tortured and spoilt rotten because of it.'

'I find it hard to picture you being the littlest.'

'There you go with the size thing again. You really do have a one-track mind, don't you?'

She laughed as she shook her head. 'You're incorrigible!'

'Yep.' He winked across the table at her. 'But at least after tonight I hope you know I can *spell* incorrigible.'

They remained in companionable silence for a few moments, their minds working on different matters. Tara spoke first. 'Why was my being in your kitchen so terrible?'

He grimaced at the question. 'Because I didn't know if you could cook?'

She blinked at him, her face deadpan.

'Not buying that one, huh?'

'Nope.'

'Okay. Damn. I guess I'd better try honesty, then.'

She nodded, her face unchanged. 'That would be nice.' Ah, that word again.

'It's a guy thing.' Pause. 'You see, a woman cooking in a man's kitchen is a domesticated scene.'

She waited.

'And it's threatening because domesticated scenes usually lead to involvement. Single guys feel threatened by that.'

'So you're a confirmed bachelor, then?'

'Is that question a trap?'

She smiled. 'I'm not here to seduce you, Jack.'

'Well, hell, why did I have a shower, then?'

'You don't think I can play this game too, do you?' She smiled. Then *nice* transformed itself miraculously into *flirtatious*. 'Cooking isn't the only thing that can be done in a kitchen with a table this size.'

Jack watched as her hand slid backwards and forwards across the table's surface. He swallowed hard. Oh, man, was he in trouble.

Suddenly domestication wasn't looking all that bad.

Tara glanced at him from beneath long eyelashes. She smiled a small smile at his flushed face. This was actually more fun that she'd anticipated.

She stood and leaned forward to lift his plate. 'Dessert?'

Jack insisted on walking her home after dinner—'In case there's still a queue...'

They stopped halfway there and sat on the grass, looking out at the water.

'So.'

She smiled, still staring forward. 'So?'

'How are we doing, here? We making some progress, do you think?'

The smile grew. 'Almost.'

'You don't know what to do about me, do you, Tara Devlin?'

She turned her head and look at his shadowed face. She didn't need light to fill in what she couldn't see. She knew how he looked now—every small line, every long lash, every fleck of colour in his eyes. It was engraved on her memory, for better or worse.

'I guess I don't—any more than you know what to do about me.'

'I don't fit into one of your preconceived boxes, that's why.'

'Right back at you, big guy.'

They both smiled, then turned back to the ocean for a few more moments, the sound of the waves filling their ears.

Jack took a breath, then dived into speech. 'What do you think other people do in this situation?'

She shrugged. 'I guess maybe they just wing it and see what happens.'

'Maybe we should try that, then.'

'Maybe.'

'I can't make you promises, Tara.'

She nodded, looking out at the dark ocean. 'That goes both ways.'

'I messed up big one time before, and I've regretted it ever since.'

'Fair enough.' It didn't take a degree in psychology to work out who he meant.

'But I can tell you I won't lie to you.'

She smiled. 'Then that's enough, I guess.'

His finger reached across, touched her chin and turned her face towards his. He studied her for a moment, then spoke with a low, seductive voice. 'I'm going to kiss you now. I'm giving you plenty of warning so you can make a get-away if you want to. Just say the word and I'll stop.'

She smiled at his reassurance. It was nice of him. Maybe this nice thing was infectious after all.

His face moved closer. 'Just tell me to stop if you don't want me to kiss you.'

She watched as he got closer.

Inches from her mouth, he whispered, 'Last chance.'

'Shut the hell up, Jack.'

His eyes closed and he moved his mouth over hers. 'Okay.'

Tara smiled against his mouth as it grew firm against hers. At least she knew where she was with this part. No surprises, no doubts, just good old-fashioned lust. She moved closer, then closer. Then as close as nature would allow without the removal of several items of clothing, her body pulled across his until she was prac-tically in his lap. This was the stuff she wrote about, but had never experienced in real life. Man, had she been tame in her descriptions.

It was like being devoured. Completely swallowed up. Every sense she possessed was tuned in to him. Smell, touch, taste—all present and correct, and desperate for more. She could feel the flame light low in her stomach, then spread across her body with the intensity of a forest fire. Every nerve-ending tingled with awareness; every muscle grew tense with anticipation.

His mouth dragged free from hers, his head dipping to her neck to allow his tongue access to the salty sea taste of her skin.

Tara moaned, a low, guttural sound in the base of her throat. 'Jack.'

His mouth curved into a smile against her neck before moving up to her ear. His low whisper tickled against her eardrum. 'Yes?'

She smiled softly. 'Nothing. Just Jack.'

He lifted his head to look down at the shadow of her face. 'Tell me you want me. Say the words so I know I'm not alone.'

She took a shaky breath, her voice falling to a whisper. 'You have to know I do. How could you not know?'

Moving large hands over her back, into her hair, he leaned down to trace her ear with his tongue, then whispered, 'I do know. But I need to hear it too.'

Her heart twisted at the combination of arrogance and insecurity. It was a potent mix to an uninitiated heart. 'I do want you.' She tangled her fingers in his short hair and pulled his head back, then kissed him before whispering, 'I guess I have done for a long time.'

He groaned, moved her further across his lap so that she could feel every inch of him, leaving no doubts as to where they were heading. His words tickled her sensitive lips. 'You see the effect you have on me?'

'Yes.' She kissed him again.

'How does knowing that make you feel?'

'It makes me feel...' She thought for a moment, moving her body slightly against his experimentally, and smiled at his sharp intake of breath. 'Like I have some control.'

'Like I'm less intimidating?'

'Jack—' She brought her head back a little to look into the dark pits of his eyes. 'If you really believe that knowing I have this effect on you will make your presence less intimidating, then you have very little insight into how intimidating pure lust can be to someone who's never experienced it before.'

He gripped his hands tighter against her back, holding her still against him, his control already tested to the limits. 'Then I guess I'll have to admit we're on common ground.'

Her breath caught in her chest. He couldn't be serious. 'You're not trying to tell me—?'

'That I've never been this instantaneously mad-as-all-hell attracted to someone in my entire life?'

She nodded.

'Do you want me to lie to you?'

'Are you?'

'No.'

She swallowed hard.

'I've been in relationships. I'm not going to pretend I haven't.'

She reminded herself to breathe in and out.

'And I'm hardly a first-timer.'

Deep, calming breaths.

'But neither have I ever met a woman who can make me want her this badly with virtually no encouragement given from her side. Until now, that is.' He smiled.

'Maybe it's that whole ''thrill of the chase'' thing?'

He leaned down to kiss her, his tongue brushing against her lips until she opened to him.

Then he raised his head again, his voice low. 'No, that's not it.'

'Then what is it?'

'Not sure.' He kissed her again. 'But I plan on finding out.'

'Maybe we should just make love and get it out of the way.'

Jack laughed, the vibration tingling against her breasts. 'And you write *what* for a living?'

She smiled in response. 'Okay, that wasn't a good example. I can do better.'

'I'm ready.'

'Yeah, I noticed.'

He laughed again. 'That's not what I meant.'

'I know.'

'You know this is verbal foreplay, right?'

'It had occurred to me.'

Sliding her body against his in an almost familiar movement, he moved his hands to her waist. He spread his palms wide against the curve, from the base of her ribcage to the top of her hips, his thumbs rubbing back and forth across the sides of her stomach.

'So, tell me what you would have said about our making love if you'd written it down in a book.'

She moistened her lips, aware that the tide was beginning to crash against the base of the cliffs. 'I'd have said, I know you want me, Jack.'

'Go on.' His hands moved upwards, his thumbs continuing their gentle strokes.

'I'd have told you that I need you to kiss me.'

He obliged. 'And then?' His thumbs brushed across the peaks of her breasts, drawing a gasp from her mouth. He began lowering his head again, slowly.

Unconsciously Tara arched her neck towards him, her head suddenly heavy. 'I'd have told you that I need you to touch me.'

'Where?' His mouth touched the inviting line of her throat.

'I believe I'd have used the word *everywhere*.'

The tide pushed harder against the rocks, stronger this time as it surrendered to the attraction of the shoreline with rhythmical waves.

After several long moments spent stealing the air from each other's lungs, he raised his head again. 'Are you stopping me this time?'

'You can stop *now*?'

CHAPTER SEVEN

Jack leaned nonchalantly against the ship's wheel as the woman glared up at him. Forgiving a long-ago mistake was never easy, and Eliza was no exception. But they had never had what he had with Catherine, and now Jack knew everything that had been lacking. Probably, deep down, Catherine was what he'd been looking for all along. He'd just never known it until now, looking at the woman who'd been so very wrong for him.

But now that he knew he realised how very lucky he was.

Eliza had been less fortunate. She'd left him as a means to an end. Marrying another man and his thousands a year had been easier than staying and waiting for Jack.

'No,' she said.

'Eliza, be reasonable.'

'That would make everything so simple for you, wouldn't it?'

A bolt of lightning appeared from the sky, killing her outright and leaving two steaming boots standing alone on the ground. Jack threw back his head and laughed and laughed and laughed...

Tara wondered if writing someone dead was considered the same as premeditated murder in a court of law. But if it was an act of God, like lightning...

She continued watching the car from her window. It had been parked outside Jack's house for over an hour now. When Sarah had emerged from the driver's seat, perfect from the top of her head to her darling stiletto-clad toes, Tara had felt a sudden need to do something to fill her time besides wondering.

Why was she there? Really? It had been as obvious as a galloping rhinoceros that Jack wanted nothing to do with her that day in the paint shop. Still, relationships were known to heal after a while. It wasn't unheard of. And Jack had said he regretted messing up...

But this was *Jack*. And, much as she hated facing up to the fact, Tara had a problem with the idea of him being wooed back by an ex. He and Sarah might have unfinished business— plenty of ex-couples did—but Tara was not a happy bunny about her being there. In truth she was a tad—jealous. And that made her mad as hell.

So she had tried writing to fill the time. Fairly soon her manuscript had been a chapter better off, but in under three-quarters of an hour she'd taken to thinking nasty thoughts. Varying types of slapstick murder had begun to enter into the storyline.

Eliza was killed again, this time by a falling balloonist on a failed attempt to float around the world. Unfortunate, really. The timeline was probably a bit out for balloons, but still…

She sipped at a cup of tea, her eyes focused again on the large windows. Just when her mind began to meander over the recent events that had led to a sudden alteration in her general feelings towards Jack, the front door to his house swung open. Ridiculously, Tara felt a sudden need to duck down behind her desk and hide.

Jack's face was unreadable from a distance. Sarah smiled sweetly up at him, then stepped closer, her head tilting as she spoke. *Cute.*

Jack glanced across at Tara's house, then Sarah stepped forward and planted an air kiss on each of his cheeks. He watched her as she stepped gracefully down the stairs towards her car. How could she do that in those heels? Then she was in her car, and with the rev of a powerful engine and a mushroom of dust along the lane she was gone.

Jack's tall frame stayed immobile as he watched the departure.

Then his eyes strayed towards Tara's house again. For a moment she even thought he might have seen her. But with a slow turn he went back inside and the door closed.

Tara watched the silent movie unfold before her, then stood up and began pacing the room. Percival watched from the sofa with narrow, perceptive eyes.

'Don't look at me like that. Yeah, okay, I know. I should just march in there and ask what the hell she was there for, right?' She sighed, her hands coming up to rest on her hips. 'If it was you you'd have wandered on over and staked your claim. Sprayed on his door or something. Well, I'm afraid that isn't exactly an option.'

She formed a mental picture of herself on Jack's porch, hackles raised as she spat at Sarah. That managed to raise a smile at least.

Jack would have found it hilarious, no doubt.

The phone rang, causing her to jump slightly. She answered it after several rings.

'Hi, honey, how was the date?'

Ah, Mags to the rescue. Tara filled her in, leaving parts of the evening sketchy, then subtly slipped in the Sarah information.

'Maybe they've decided to be friends.'

'Yeah, that's likely. I can see that from how well they got on in the paint shop.'

'Honey, they obviously got on at some point.' Mags was adept at pointing out the obvious. 'Maybe she left some belongings with him that she had to collect.'

'That fitted in her left ear? There was no room to carry anything else in what she was wearing.'

'She was just passing?'

Tara smiled. 'Nice try, but I don't think Ross's Point has the same postcode as ''just passing''.'

Mags sighed. 'Well, hell, I don't know, do I? Why don't you try something outrageous and off-the-wall like—ooh—asking him?'

'No can do.'

'Because that might give an indication that you care? And we all know what a horribly immature idea that would be, right?'

Tara lifted the phone from her ear, frowned at it, then set it back. 'OK, I will admit that I am possibly being a little teeny bit immature about this—'

'Not to mention jealous as hell.'

'You can stop enjoying this any time soon.'

'I'll keep that in mind.'

'You may be slightly right.' Tara grimaced at the admission. 'But it's not like I'm his girlfriend or anything. I've known him about five minutes, and one evening of getting along hardly makes for a lifetime commitment.'

Mags laughed on the other end of the line. 'Oh, sweetie, this is better than one of your books—really. Reading between the lines, I'd say there was a damn sight more than ''getting along'' going on last night.'

Tara felt her cheeks burn. 'I don't kiss and tell.'

'You mentioned kissing, so there's *something* to tell. So did you?'

'Did I what?'

'You know.'

'Would I ask if I did?'

'Simple answer: yes or no.'

'No, Mags.'

'No, you're not telling me? Or no, you didn't?'

'Why don't you just fill in the gaps?'

'Isn't that Jack's job?'

She shook her head. 'This is all your fault, you know. You and your great ''Jack is my hero'' thing.'

'Ah, now, that's not exactly what I said. I merely hinted that maybe he was closer to your ideal than you were letting yourself see.'

'I will reluctantly admit that there's more to him than I originally thought.'

'Hero material?'

'Not if he's hanging around with his ex, no.'

'Then ask him.'

'I hate you.'

It was almost too easy when it came down to it.

'Sarah came to see me.'

'Mmm, I noticed.'

Jack glanced at her from the corner of his eye. 'Were you spying?'

'That would make it seem like I have a life, wouldn't it?'

He grinned. 'I wouldn't mind. It'd show you were interested.'

She turned to look at him, her paintbrush poised in mid-air. 'Would you prefer it if I went back to ignoring you?'

'Hell, no.' Blue eyes locked with grey. 'I much prefer the sparring. It gets better results.' He winked. Tara felt a blush climb over her cheeks.

'Yeah, well, you just remember that the next time we have an argument.'

'The fact that I enjoy the sparring, or the results?'

The blush gained momentum. 'You're not a nice person.'

He dipped his roller back into a tray of paint, avoiding her eyes. 'So, you want to hear about it this time?'

She studied his profile for a second. 'Not if you don't want to tell me.' *Liar.*

He took a deep breath, the roller stationary for a moment, inches from the bare wall. 'Is that a trap? You know—the kind of thing where no matter what answer I give I'm still in trouble?'

Tara took extra-special care around a light switch, tracing the edges with her narrow paintbrush. He was right to a certain extent. 'If it's a personal thing then I'll understand your not wanting to talk about it.' *Liar, liar, pants on fire.*

'And you'll be okay with that?'

A small smile crossed her lips. 'Not entirely, no.'

Covering the roller with paint again, he brushed it over the wall in smooth strokes. 'So what we're saying here, basically, is that I can't win. If I tell you and you're not happy with what you hear then you'll flip—'

'I'll *flip*?'

He held the roller in front of him like a truce flag. 'I'll rephrase that. You'll be annoyed.'

'Better.' She frowned at him. 'Though, just so you know, I don't like that description much either. It suggests I'm temperamental.'

He hid a smile, shrugging instead, the material of his blue denim shirt stretching across his chest with the movement. 'But you will be, right?'

She carefully removed her paintbrush from the wall, turning to face him with a slight tilt of her chin. 'There is that possibility.'

Blue eyes softened at her expression. With a smile to match he answered, 'I'd have been disappointed if you hadn't, actually. It shows you give a damn.'

There was a moment of silence, then they returned to the wall. The sound of paint sticking to the dry surface filled the silence for several minutes, then, 'So, you had a visitor?'

'Yes, I did.'

'And what was she like?'

'About five foot eight.'

'Funny.'

'I thought so.'

Tara simmered silently as she continued up the edge of the door panel. 'Fine, don't tell me. It was you who brought it up in the first place.'

'See—there it is.' He turned to look at her. 'The trap. I knew it was there. Why don't you just say what's on your mind and then I won't have to pretend to be psychic?'

'And Mags thinks *I'm* defensive?'

'Was that aimed at me?' He blinked. 'Are you suggesting that *I'm* being defensive?'

Tara stared up at him, realisation kicking into action in her brain. 'You are, aren't you? That's what half of this is about.'

'Nope, you've lost me.' He wiped his hands on a rag and walked into the hallway to search for more paint, throwing words over his shoulder as he went. 'I haven't the faintest idea what you mean.'

She followed, wiping her hands on the same rag. 'That's it, isn't it?'

'What's it?'

'All these arguments—all this stuff that we throw at each other. It's not just me being defensive, is it?'

Looking at the patchy ceiling, he took a deep breath, his hands on his hips. 'What do you want now? An award?'

She stared at the broad expanse of his back, her mouth open. It was something she just hadn't expected, hadn't looked for. In Jack, of all people. He just seemed so self-assured all the time. 'Why?'

'Why would you want an award?' He turned his head to glance over his shoulder. 'For being smart enough to figure out I'm human too? Is that such a big shocker? Maybe you should ring the tabloids, get it out in the open: *Chink found in Neanderthal man's armour.*'

'Actually, they didn't have armour then. Mostly fur off dead things, I believe.'

Jack shook his head, continuing down the wide staircase with bouncing steps. His voice echoed in the empty rooms above and below. 'You're just trying to deflect attention away from the fact that you're jealous.'

'The hell I am!'

'Careful with those insults, sweetheart, you'll hurt my feelings.'

'You see—you're doing it again.' She smiled as she put it together in her mind. 'You're trying to goad me into losing my temper so we can get off the subject of *you*.'

'If you say so it must be true.' His voice sounded from a room downstairs. 'But you *are* annoyed that Sarah was here.'

'I didn't say I wasn't.'

The house was silent for a couple of minutes. Tara stood at the top of the stairs, listening carefully for movement. Or breathing. Life of any kind, in fact. When she heard nothing she smiled again, imagining the look on his face as he tried to avoid her questioning.

'Percival suggested I should mark my territory on your doorstep, but I thought that would be taking things a bit far.'

Still the silence remained.

'So I killed off the other Jack's ex a couple of dozen ways to fill in the time. Some of them were fairly gruesome murders, I can tell you.'

She thought she heard a footstep, and stretched her neck to look over the banister. 'Are you going to hide down there all day, or are you going to be a man about this?'

A woman's voice answered. 'I try my best *not* to be a man about things. Men can be so wrong most of the time.'

Tara gaped at the gorgeous creature standing at the bottom of the stairs, running a paint-smeared hand unconsciously through her own untidy blonde tresses.

'Uh—hi, there.'

The woman grinned. 'Hi, there, to you. And you are?'

'Tara?'

'Tara painter and decorator? Tara the handy-person? Tara the—'

'You'll never get her to admit to anything.' Jack appeared at the woman's side. 'Believe me, I've tried.' He glared up the stairway. 'Tara—my sister Rachel. Rachel—' He waved a hand upwards. 'Tara—the woman who's going to send me to the nut house.'

'Nice to meet you.' Rachel's grin widened as she turned to look at her brother. 'About time too.' Her eyes sparkled back at Tara. 'So, who's for coffee, then?'

Jack risked an upward glance at Tara as Rachel moved towards the kitchen. He frowned at her scowling face. 'Not my fault this time.'

'Convenient, though,' she snapped at him as she came down the stairs. 'This isn't over, so don't think it is.'

He caught her arm as she tried to walk past him, drawing her to him and pressing a searing, mind-numbing kiss on her lips. When he eventually released her he smiled down at her stunned expression.

'Sometimes that's the only way I can think of to get you to stop arguing with me.'

She raised her chin haughtily, tugging her arm free. 'Well, maybe if you did it a bit more often I wouldn't get so carried away.'

There was another sister in the kitchen, this one slightly smaller than the other one, with fairer hair and an openly friendly face. 'Hi— Tara, isn't it?'

Tara accepted the hand that was offered in her direction. 'Hi.'

'I'm Lauren, Jack's—'

'Sister, yeah.' She started unzipping the front of the overalls Jack had given her for painting service. Not that four sizes too big wasn't extremely flattering, but a girl had to do something when surrounded by all these beautiful people. Her hand went to her hair again.

Jack caught the self-conscious movement from his position at the other side of the kitchen. He smiled, which caught Lauren's attention and earned an answering smile in his direction. He stuck his tongue out at her.

'So, how long have you known the Squirt, then?'

Tara started to grin. 'The Squirt?'

'That lump over there.' Rachel nodded her head in Jack's direction. 'It was his nickname growing up. It's funnier now, though.'

Her smile grew as she looked across at him. 'Yeah, it is.'

He shook his head, leaning back against the counter, arms folded across his chest. 'Hilarious. You guys bring the naked baby photos with you too?'

'Damn, no, I didn't.' Rachel clicked her fingers. 'You, Lauren?'

'No, they're in my other bag.'

'Shame. So, what were you two arguing about?' Rachel focused on Tara. 'It sounded like an interesting debate.'

'Rach, butt out.'

She ignored Jack's thunderous look with a wave of one hand, pulling out a chair at the table with the other. 'Ignore him. He makes a lot of noise but it's all show. He's a little fluffy kitten, really.'

Tara sat down with a broad grin. 'I can't say I'd noticed that.'

'Oh, you'll get it when you've been around him as long as we have.'

The back door opened and yet another sister appeared. This one was familiar, with a mop of madly curling hair. Her blue eyes landed on Tara. 'Who's this?' She kissed Jack's cheek before grabbing a cup and pouring coffee at his side. 'Is this the writer?'

Tara raised an eyebrow in Jack's direction. He smiled sheepishly. 'Yes, that's her.'

'Well, you're right. She's no grandmother.'

Jack took a deep breath. 'To what do I owe this honour?'

'Family forum.' Lauren handed a cup to Tara. 'Tess called it. It's Dad's birthday arrangements.'

Jack's nodded. 'Of course it is. And it didn't occur to anyone to maybe phone first?'

Tara glanced around the room as all eyes landed on Jack. She tried to stand up. 'You guys have family stuff to discuss so I'll just go—'

Rachel tugged her back into her seat. 'Not 'til after you've had a coffee and told all us all about the conversation you were having when we arrived. I don't think I can stand the suspense, and Jack gets all upset when we ask him private stuff.'

Tara raised her chin with a smug smile for Jack. 'Oh, is that so?'

'You *cannot* use that as evidence for the prosecution.'

'I think you'll find I can.'

'No, it's circumstantial. You only have her to believe.' He pointed a long finger at Rachel.

'And me. I agree with that statement.' Lauren joined Tara's team.

'Thanks,' said Jack.

'Which part of the statement are we talking about?' Tess sat down opposite Tara, her eyes searching the younger woman's face with caution, or possibly suspicion. 'Bring me up to speed.'

'Jack and Tara were having an argument when we arrived.'

'It wasn't quite an argument—'

'More of a debate—'

They smiled across at each other as they spoke at the same time. Then Jack looked at his sisters. 'Haven't you heard of the word *private*?'

'Wasn't it on that scrap of paper you used to pin to your bedroom door?'

'He probably had writer's cramp from the number of times he had to replace that sign.' Lauren grinned. 'He gave up after a couple of weeks.'

Rachel smiled at Tara. '*You* can tell us to get lost if you like. But when you're family you just learn to suffer, I'm afraid.' She blew a kiss at her brother.

'So, you were arguing?' Tess continued, studying Tara with guarded eyes. 'Does that happen much?'

'It wasn't an argument.' Jack jumped to Tara's defence. 'So lay off. We just…' his eyes swept across to meet hers '…have this verbal sparring thing that we do.'

Tara blushed faintly and hid in her coffee cup.

'Do you, now? Do tell.'

'We just don't always see eye to eye so we…debate.'

'Until you both agree?'

'No.' His eyes sparkled. 'Not always.'

Tara's face grew warmer as she felt four sets of blue eyes land on her. She reappeared from the depths of her cup. 'We were just talking about how defensive Jack can be.'

'Tell me about it.'

'You're not joking there.'

Jack groaned. 'Great—that's terrific. You fairer sex always stick together, don't you?'

Tara watched as he lifted his cup and walked across the kitchen. 'And then what he does is walk away rather than admit I'm right.'

He stopped. 'I do no such thing, and unless you want me to tell this lot exactly what I do to end the debate then I suggest you stop right there.'

'I'm right this time, though.'

'Tara.'

The sisters watched as Jack faced off against Tara across the table, his expression thunderous. Tara simply raised her chin, folding her arms across her chest. *'Jack.'*

Rachel grinned. 'Oh, I'm loving this. Jack's finally met his match.'

'Rachel!'

'You needn't pull that tough act on me either, Squirt. I know you better.' She winked at Tara. 'And we all know you can be defensive as hell when it comes to anything resembling how you might actually feel about something.'

Jack looked upwards. 'And I keep moving around to avoid you guys because…?'

'And that's a *whole* other issue, isn't it?'

Tess, who had remained silent for most of the discussion, finally leaned forward in her chair. 'Does it matter to you that he's defensive? That maybe he might have a reason for it?'

Tara's grey eyes widened at the direct question. If Jack had asked it she would more than likely have danced around the answer for a while, but somehow, in a small way, it seemed important she was straight with Tess. 'Yes—I think it does, actually.'

'Why?'

Jack watched her, his breath held still in his wide chest.

Tara continued to hold Tess's steady gaze. 'Because, despite my better judgement, it would appear I'm starting to like him. Though I'm still holding out hope that I may get over it.'

His breath came out in a silent whoosh. Then a grin appeared. 'You'd never have admitted that to *me* in a million years.'

She shrugged. '*You* didn't ask me.' Her eyes met his for a second. 'Anyway, it would take an idiot not to have figured that out by now, and we're both aware that you may be many things but dumb isn't one of them.'

'Another compliment.'

Tess leaned back in her chair again. 'What brought about this debate in the first place?'

Tara's eyes moved back to her face. 'He's always accusing me of being defensive, and I just figured out today that it's not just me doing it.'

'You're defensive too?'

'A little.' She sighed at Jack's snort of derision. 'Okay, a lot. But he can just rub you up the wrong way so quickly. Arrogant, overbearing, patronising—in fact a right royal pain in the—'

'They already know.'

The women nodded in agreement.

'Well, you know what I mean, then. Half the time you just want to kill him—'

'And the other half?' His grin remained.

Tara pointed up at him. 'See what I mean?'

Rachel jerked her head in Tara's direction as she smiled at her brother. 'I like her.'

He nodded. 'Me too. I think I'll let her stay a while.'

'I live next door, so you don't actually have a big choice in that.'

Tess smiled a small, wistful smile. 'Don't be so sure. He has this habit of disappearing.'

'I've never left the country.'

Tara searched his face as he looked down at Tess. 'Maybe I'll find out the reason for all that at some stage too.'

'Oh, *that*.' Rachel turned to face her. 'That's easy, it's all because of—Ow!'

Tess glared at her sister. 'I'm sure if Jack wants Tara to know he'll tell her himself.'

Rachel looked at Tess, then up at Jack. 'Okay, you're right.'

Tara smiled encouragingly when Rachel looked at her again. 'Don't worry, it's half the fun—wheedling information out of each other. Otherwise we might never have anything to talk about.'

They were distracted by another set of footsteps. A voice sounded in the hallway. 'Jack? Guys? Tess said something about Sarah being back—'

Tara's eyes shot back to Jack as the final sister joined them. His face was impassive when she'd expected—what? A look of guilt? An apologetic glance? Jealousy reared its ugly head again and she dropped her chin to hide it.

With a pang of regret at having to leave the warmth of family banter and the opportunity to find out about the elusive Sarah, she stood and made her excuses. Lauren and Rachel stood too,

Rachel reaching forward to envelop Tara in a hug. 'It's been lovely meeting you. Hopefully we'll get to see you again soon.'

Tara blushed as they parted. 'Thanks.' She smiled at the others as she backed away. 'Well, I'll leave you to it.'

Jack walked outside the door with her. 'We'll talk later, okay?'

'That would be okay.' If he wanted to tell her about Sarah, he would. Tara knew that much. No one with this warm a family could be all bad, could they? She crossed her fingers at her side.

He smiled, the warmth reaching all the way up to his eyes. 'Good.'

And suddenly she was reassured.

It was dark by the time her door opened.

'Hey.' She smiled up at him from the sofa.

Jack ran long fingers through his short hair, spiking it ridiculously. 'Hey to you too.' With a tired smile he lifted her legs and sat down, setting her legs across his thighs. 'Did you eat yet?'

'Snacked.' She examined his face for a moment. 'How's you?'

'Tired.'

A smile appeared, dimples creasing his cheeks as he rested his head against the back of the sofa, his eyes focused on hers. 'I look that good, do I?'

Well, actually… 'You look okay. Just tired.'

'I had too many women making me think today. That's rough going, you know.'

'I'll bet.' She smiled back at him. 'Poor you.'

He reached a hand out to smooth a lock of hair back from her cheek. For a few moments he was silent, a variety of unreadable thoughts crossing his eyes, then he seemed to make a decision. 'Sarah came to see me.'

'I got that.' She reached up to her cheek and twined her fingers with his before setting their hands back in her lap and studying the differences in the male and female hand. It was quite sexy, actually.

He took a breath. 'I know you probably think that means something. That there must be a reason after all this time.'

'Could be.' She continued her scientific study.

'And I could just tell you nothing and have you work it up into some great big thing in your head.'

Tara meshed her fingers in and out of his. 'I have a very active imagination.'

He smirked. 'Occasionally that talent has its place.'

She felt her cheeks warm. 'You have such a one-track mind.'

He studied her face, waiting for her to look over at him. The smart-ass answers were all too easy for him, but this was important. Reassuring Tara was important. It was something new to him. A tad scary, truth be told.

He looked deep into her eyes, as if searching her soul for some reassurance of his own. Of what? That it mattered to her that he wasn't messing with another woman? That she was even the slightest bit jealous? With a blink of his own eyes he knew the answers to both were yes. And that was about as big a revelation as he needed just yet.

'There's nothing going on that you need to worry about.'

Except that Sarah had been there in the first place. Except that Tara didn't know what was going on between them. She didn't know the history of their relationship, or if they could mend it.

And she didn't know what this newly discovered warmth she felt in her chest when Jack looked at her that certain way meant. The way he was looking at her right that minute.

'Okay.'

'Okay?'

He blinked at her, his gaze steady, opened his mouth as if to add something, then looked away from her, his eyes searching the room. 'Can I make us coffee or something?' He moved her legs again, pushing himself up into a standing position. 'Or maybe you're hungry?'

She watched patiently as he moved into the kitchen, filling the kettle with his back to her. It was funny how easy it suddenly was: the massive shift in their relationship that so short a while ago she had thought was impossible. When she had more time to herself she would maybe worry a little more about how quickly it had happened.

Swinging her legs over, she sat upright. 'Are you avoiding me again?'

He didn't turn to face her. 'I went as far as the kitchen. That's not that big a journey.'

'No, but it's what you're doing, isn't it? You're distancing yourself from me. If I was paranoid, I'd worry there was something behind that.'

'Are you paranoid?'

'Me?' She shrugged her shoulders. 'No more than any other female—possibly a tad more seven days out of twenty-eight.' Her eyes studied the set of his shoulders. 'I just think you find it easier to walk away or avoid things that might be—I don't know—emotional, than stand still to look at them closer.' Taking a breath, she waded further into deep waters. 'It's possibly the reason you keep moving locations too.'

He clapped his hands slowly as he turned to face her with a sarcastic smile. 'Well, congratulations. A writer *and* a psychoanalyst.'

Tara raised her chin a defensive notch. 'And now you're being cruel, because that's easier than talking about it.'

His hands stopped mid-clap, then slowly went back to his sides. 'It must be tough being right all the time.'

'It would be if I was, but we're both aware that I'm not.'

'You think I'm pushing you away?'

She smiled a small smile. 'I think you're trying to.'

'Is it working?'

The smile grew. 'Apparently not.'

An answering smile began in his eyes. 'What did I do to deserve that?'

She stood up and began to walk across to him on silent, reindeer-clad feet. 'The jury's still out on that one.'

They met on either side of the breakfast bar. Jack studied her face, from the errant lock of blonde hair that shone in the lamplight to the soft line of her mouth. His heart beat hard in his chest. 'If I ask you to be a little patient with me on this stuff, you can ask me something in return. How does that sound?'

'It sounds okay.'

Leaning across the wooden surface, he raised her chin with one long finger before brushing his mouth across hers. 'Ask away, then.'

Don't break my heart, Jack.

She smiled, her eyes hooded. 'Where's my coffee?'

CHAPTER EIGHT

JACK paced the floor in his kitchen. There was still what was left of a large bouquet of mixed flowers plastered across his front door. He knew in the back of his mind that he should clear it up before anyone saw it.

Who was he kidding? Before *Tara* saw it. She would want to know why it was there and he was still above admitting his shortcomings to her. He was damned if he'd let go of his pride.

It had seemed a vaguely romantic gesture, picking up the flowers on his way out because he'd been thinking about her. But in hindsight he should probably have thought more about how the morning's meeting would affect him and his temper levels.

It just would have been so much simpler if she'd stayed away. Sarah. How could he have been so blind to her? She'd seemed the perfect woman. Beautiful, ambitious. She had fitted in with the life he'd had then. But he hadn't been happy in that life, and when the cracks had started to show and he'd made changes the cracks had grown wider in their relationship—until eventually he'd realised it just wasn't for him. In the process he'd hurt her badly. Something he'd never intended to do.

He had consoled his conscience with the fact that it had been the honourable thing to do. That it was better to break up than spend his life living a lie. They were completely and utterly incompatible at the end. How were they supposed to overcome that? He had felt she deserved better than that—didn't she? Didn't they both? By breaking up he'd given her a chance at what she deserved. It wasn't his fault it hadn't worked.

Hell hath no fury…

His eyes searched the room around him, desperate for something to focus his anger on. Unfortunately the kitchen was the one room he'd made the most headway in. With long strides he made his way into the hall.

She had still been his fiancée when he'd set up the company with Adam, when he'd bought his first house and begun the work on it that had turned him a profit and allowed him to buy the next. He'd got onto the ladder and by the third house he'd been able to buy it outright—no mortgage.

Now she said she was entitled to half of everything and she was suing him. Even though he'd more than paid back what little she'd put in in furniture, décor and time. It was the least he'd felt he could do then, but it had never completely eased his sense of guilt. And now she wanted more—much more.

Any wonder that men stayed clear of women and attachment? He'd worked for years to have financial security, to owe nothing to anyone. To have pride in himself again.

His footsteps echoed in the hallway as he looked from empty room to empty room. Finally his eyes fell on the covered-up fireplace in the dining room.

That would do.

The first thud of the sledgehammer was immensely satisfying. Stopping to remove his sweater, he swung again.

'That's for my being stupid enough to believe you could actually be a remotely understanding woman.'

A shower of plasterboard exploded from the next impact.

'That's for not listening to Adam and not making you sign a piece of paper when I gave you all that money the first time.' A billow of dust mushroomed upwards into the air. 'Money I didn't damn well have to give you...'

Another echoing thud. 'And that's for screwing up my perception of relationships to such an extent that I can't get my head round them any more.'

He set the hammer-head on the ground for a moment and rubbed dust from his eyes, then swung again with a grunt of effort. 'That's for—'

'Can I join in? Or is this a solo effort?'

The hammer-head hit the floor again. Turning slowly, he found Tara leaning against the doorframe. 'How long have you been there?'

'Pretty much since your first attack on that poor, innocent wall.'

Jack nodded. 'Figures.' He didn't even want to think about the things his statements had revealed to her.

'I take it you saw Sarah again?'

He smiled sarcastically. 'Yeah, we had another little reunion.'

She sighed quietly, despite a small sense of relief at his reaction. 'Not good, I take it?'

He turned away and swung the hammer at the wall again. A hole appeared in the centre of the fireplace. 'You could say that.'

'Want to tell me?'

'No, not yet. I'm still too wound up.'

'I got that from the flowers on your front door.'

He glanced over his shoulder. 'Those were for you.'

'Thanks.' She smiled. 'I'll peel them off later.'

The swinging motion of the hammer was stilled when Tara wound her arms around his waist, pressing her body along the length of his back.

Jack set the hammer down, setting one hand on top of the clasped hands on his belt buckle. 'My anger management needs a little working on.'

'Well, you are currently a work in progress.'

He smiled. 'Am I? And you are…?'

'A calming influence in your life?' She rested her cheek against his back, smoothing her skin against the warmth that radiated through his shirt. 'At present, I hope, anyway. At least for the sake of your load-bearing walls.'

He let the hammer's wooden handle drop to the floor, turning around to pull her into his arms. 'I wouldn't have used the word *calming*.'

'Really?' She raised an eyebrow, her eyes sparkling. 'What word would you have used?'

He dipped his head to hers, stealing the breath from her mouth as he claimed her lips. The tension and anger that had had his body taut as a bowstring immediately transformed into wanting, a need for release of a different kind. He felt her melt against him, her body moulding to him in all the right places. With a smile against her mouth he realised that even though their confusing relationship was growing and changing every day, the sexual spark between them refused to die down. If anything, it was stronger than before.

She smiled back against his lips, refusing to break away as she continued speaking to him. 'Something funny…Squirt?'

He kissed her quickly, talking back in the same way, with his mouth against hers. 'No, not a thing.'

Another kiss. 'Then what's with the smile?'

'I guess…' *Kiss*. '…I must…' *Kiss, kiss.* '…like being around you.' *Kiss.*

She laughed. 'Ditto.'

He looked down into her eyes, so close to his, as he backed them towards a wall. 'This kind of thing makes up for a really bad day.'

She continued speaking between kisses. 'Glad to be of service.'

Unwinding his arms from around her waist, he brought his hands up to free her hair from its plait. His long fingers tangled through the soft strands as he continued showering her with small kisses. 'I missed you.'

She went still, blinking as she strained to hear the whispered words. 'What did you say?'

He raised his head a small inch. 'Who? Me?'

'No, the third guy in the queue waiting to kiss me.'

He grinned. 'Tell him to wait his turn.' Another kiss, then he moved his head downward, using the fingers in her hair to tilt her head back, baring her slender throat to his mouth. 'I could be here a while.'

Tara mulled over what she'd heard him saying as she entered the room. In a way she felt closer to him, having witnessed his rare vulnerability. She wouldn't push him to repeat the words she was so sure she'd heard. It was time for a little patience.

'Maybe I should get a chair, then.' She moaned softly as his tongue brushed over her skin. 'In case my legs get tired.'

He continued down the line of her throat as he felt the soft thud of her back hitting the wall. 'I can help out with that.' He moved a hand, lifting one of her denim-clad legs and wrapping it around his waist. Swapping hands, he did the same with her other leg. 'See?'

She looked up into his smiling face with heavily hooded eyes. 'Should I check the hallway for sisters before we get caught up in the moment?'

He laughed. 'You're safe.'

Actually, she was well past the stage of safe. She glanced over his shoulder. 'No unexpected visitors, then?'

'No one to rescue you, no.'

'Do I need rescuing?'

'From me?' He rocked his hips against her. 'Or from the here and now?'

'From you.' The words were out before she could disguise them with witty repartee. So much for patience. She avoided his eyes, burying her mouth against the crook of his neck, her tongue touching against the salt of his skin to distract him. 'And, of course, from all these dangerous things you make me feel.'

He ignored the teasing in her voice and focused instead on the look she'd had in her eye when she'd said, *'From you.'* With a slight reorganisation of her light weight, he cupped her behind with one arm, and used the other in her hair to lift her face again. 'What are you scared of?'

'Me?'

'No, the guy in the queue.'

She tried to avoid his piercing stare but found her head put back into place with a firm hand. 'The usual stuff, like spiders, mice—that kind of thing.'

His eyes sparked with anger. 'I've heard enough crap today, Tara.'

'So you want what, exactly?' Her eyes sparked in return, a spasm cramping her stomach. 'Honesty? Is that what you're looking for?'

'Didn't I make a promise about that?'

He had. Technically speaking, she hadn't. She had decided that if he could give a little, so could she. But that was before she'd got so involved. Before she'd stood a very real chance of having her heart broken.

'You want me to go out on a limb when you can't?'

He studied her face carefully. 'Maybe one of us should.'

Fine. He wanted to open the can of worms, add to the problems of the day? Then she'd damn well open it for him.

'I'm scared stiff I'm falling for you, scared of what letting go could mean.'

The fingers in her hair stilled, then moved more gently, beginning a kneading motion against the back of her head.

She blinked as her eyes welled. 'I'm scared that one tomorrow you'll be gone, and I'll have opened up Pandora's box only to be proved right for never having allowed any man to get that close before.'

Jack looked down on her face and felt that his chest would crush his heart. He was already involved with her more than he'd wanted to be. Now, suddenly, he felt a wave of protectiveness towards her—a need to reassure her and tell her they'd be all right. But he couldn't do that, could he? There weren't any guarantees with him. He'd already proved that once.

With a moment of hesitation, he leaned down to capture her mouth again, his words tickling against her swollen lips. 'I'm not going anywhere.'

She wrapped her arms tighter around his neck, as if by holding on with all her physical strength she could bind him to her. Make truth of his words.

Her hunger matched his as they tangled with mouths and tongues and limbs. It was just too late for her now. The way he was worming his way into her heart every single day was more than she could fight off. She was just going to have to go out on that damned limb and hope the excess weight of her emotions didn't prove too heavy for it to hold.

'It's nice to see someone happy.'

Tara glanced up at Sheila Mitchell's open, friendly face. 'Me?'

Sheila glanced around the small store. 'Well, I don't see anyone else.' Her eyes locked with Tara's. 'Funny thing too. You're the second person I've seen today with that particular look. Must be the day for it.'

Tara's smile grew broader. 'Really? And who might that have been?'

'Oh, I think we both know.'

'Mmm.'

Sheila followed her between the rows of shelving. 'Well, I think it's nice. You could do with someone. And he is easy on the eye. I promise not to mention it to the ladies, though.'

She tapped the side of her nose. 'Your secret's safe with me.'

The bell above the shop door jingled loudly and a blast of cool air entered. Tara's gaze followed Sheila's to the doorway, and her eyes widened in surprise at the unwanted familiarity of Sarah's face.

Her cool eyes registered recognition. 'Well, this is nice. It's Jack's friend.'

'Sarah.'

'And you remember my name.' She lifted an already arched eyebrow. 'That's sweet of you. I'm glad I popped in.'

To hell with nice.

Sheila cleared her throat gently.

Tara glanced at her and then remembered her manners. 'I'm sorry. Sarah, this is Sheila Mitchell—Sheila owns the store. Sheila, this is...' She searched for appropriate words. 'Someone Jack knew from a while back. Sarah...?'

Sarah's expression had remained cool throughout the introductions. Now she nodded in Sheila's direction, her eyes remaining on Tara. 'Fitzgerald. Interesting description you chose—very subtle, non-committal.' A small smile touched her mouth. 'I'm so sorry, I can't remember your name. What was it again?'

'Tara.'

'Oh, yes, that's it. I remember now.' She set her keys onto the counter-top, smiling dazzlingly at Sheila. 'I'm absolutely dreadful with names. Never forget a face, but names always manage to escape me.'

Sheila smiled in return. 'I have an old aunt who's exactly the same.'

Laughter danced into the air. 'Isn't it awful? And it makes me seem *so* rude.' She placed a hand on Tara's forearm. 'I do hope you'll forgive me, Tara. I just know I'll remember you now that I've met you a second time. By the next time we meet we'll practically be old friends.'

Tara smiled weakly, feeling as if she'd just been swept along on a huge wave of nasty-nice. She was vaguely nauseous from the journey. 'Are you here to visit Jack again?'

Sarah sighed, her hand squeezing Tara's arm before she released it. 'Well, since I'm in the neighbourhood. It can be awkward sometimes, but I think we're getting somewhere.' She swept a look at Sheila. 'You know how it can be with exes...'

Sheila's eyes widened. 'Well, yes—it can be awkward sometimes, I guess.' She stared at Tara. 'Don't you think, Tara?'

'I wouldn't know, I'm sure.' She moved her shopping basket to the till. 'I lead that sheltered a life I never get much of a chance to bump into the army of exes I have secreted around the countryside.'

Sarah laughed again. 'Well, I can see why Jack gets along with you. You have exactly his sense of humour. It was one of the things I liked first about him too, so I can see you and I will get along famously.'

Tara smiled weakly. *When they sell ice cream in hell, honey.*

Sheila watched this interaction with a slight twitch at the corners of her mouth. 'I'm sure Jack will be glad to see a—uh—friend.'

Oh, yeah, ecstatic. Tara hoped, with a knot forming in her belly, that he'd forgotten where the sledgehammer was.

Sarah sighed slightly. 'We'll see.'

'Has it been long since you broke up?'

Tara stared at Sheila as if she was an alien. Which in many ways she was to Tara. She would never have asked a question like that— or any of the others she was fairly sure would follow, judging by the glint in Sheila's eyes. Tara's modus operandi was more low-key than that. Like, for instance, not asking at all and then assuming the worst. It had always worked for her. But on this occasion she already knew there was a 'worst' somewhere.

'It's been a while.'

Sarah had answered her. Tara's eyes were drawn back to the woman who had once held Jack's heart. Her stomach churned. There it was again—the green-eyed monster. They were nearly friends now.

'Do you see him much now?'

'No, I can't say I do. Though it may be a great deal more in the next few weeks.'

As if at a tennis match, Tara's head followed the conversation backwards and forwards.

Sarah smiled warmly at her. 'I've been thinking about him a lot recently.'

'Oh?' Tara stunned herself with her own sparkling repartee.

'Well, you know how it can be with... unfinished business.' She continued smiling. 'So I thought it best that I just bite the bullet and see if we can't at the very least manage a civil conversation. What do *you* think?'

'Me?' She blinked wide eyes. 'Oh, I hardly ever think at all. I find it tiring.'

Sheila smiled broadly.

'Oh, I'm sure that's not true.' A bubble of musical laughter danced through the air. 'You can't make your living as a writer if you're not an intelligent woman to begin with.'

Tara's eyes were looking upwards, mentally following the pathway of that musical laughter. She refocused, her brain kicking into gear. 'I don't remember telling you I write.'

'Didn't you?' Sarah blinked. 'Oh, well, I guess Jack must have mentioned it when he was chatting about guests for his father's birthday.'

'*You're* going to his father's birthday celebration?'

A slow smile appeared. 'Of course I am.' Sarah sighed, glancing across at Sheila. 'The thing is, for a long time they were my family too. I couldn't have stayed away when he asked me to go with him.'

Tara gritted her teeth. 'Of course you couldn't.'

The front door swung open.

Jack watched as Tara walked into the hallway, sunlight at her back and glinting in her hair. She glanced in his direction, then continued walking. Removing the dust mask from his face, he followed her.

'Hey.'

'Hey.' Her voice sounded from across the hall.

Setting the electric sander down, he walked into the hall, his eyes searching from side to side. 'You okay?'

'Uh-huh—fine. I knocked, but you didn't hear me over your thingy.'

Following the sound of her voice, he found her in the dining room, her hands on her hips as she glanced around the room.

'Yeah, it's a fairly noisy thingy when it's going. Are you sure you're okay?'

She stepped towards him, her eyes glancing into his for a split second. 'Yep.'

Jack stood statue-still as she reached around him to retrieve the sledgehammer from its resting place against the wall. He watched as she swung it with all her might towards the hole in the fireplace. Dust spiralled upwards, twinkling in the sunlight.

'Well, if you're sure…'

She swung again. 'Oh, I'm just getting better by the second.'

His patience was rewarded after a third swing. She turned towards him and bestowed on him one of her most dazzling smiles. With a newly familiar grip to his chest, he smiled back.

Stepping closer, she stood on her trainer-clad toes and kissed him, before handing him the hammer. 'Thanks.'

He followed her like a sheep as she walked back down the hall. 'You want to tell me what that was all about?'

She smiled sweetly over her shoulder. 'Oh, I'm sure you'll know soon enough.'

'We're still on for Dad's birthday thing later?'

'Oh, yes, wouldn't miss it for millions,' she answered in a sing-song voice, and the front door closed.

Invite two of them at once? Tara knew better... Literary murders awaited.

Jack continued smiling affectionately. 'Still a nutcase, though.'

The family get-together was vastly different from the one Tara had experienced two days ago. This time there was far less of the affectionate bantering she had witnessed and a very noticeable something in the air. Jack stuck to her like glue. It was endearing—or would have been if she hadn't at times felt like a shield for him to hide behind.

Dana, the youngest of the sisters, eventually sidled up to Tara at the buffet laid out on Rachel's huge kitchen table. 'Hi, there. We didn't get to meet the other day. I'm Dana.'

Tara balanced her plate in one hand and shook the hand offered to her. 'Hi.'

'A little tense tonight, isn't it?'

'Can't say I'd noticed,' Tara lied, then smiled when Dana raised a disbelieving eyebrow. 'Okay, that was a fib. Though you using the word ''little'' was a bit of a fib too.'

'Yes, it was.'

They smiled at each other. Dana spooned some salad onto her plate as they worked their way down the table. 'Was Jack very awful yesterday? I'll bet he was like a bear when he got home.'

'He was…tense.'

'Mmm.'

Tara glanced through the large archway that separated the kitchen from the living room. Jack and Tess were standing by the windows, heads bowed in low conversation. From the set of

Jack's jawline she could tell he wasn't particularly happy with the topic.

'He didn't talk about it much.' She turned and smiled an almost apologetic smile. 'It really isn't any of my business, after all.'

'Oh, I think it is, in a way.'

Tara raised an eyebrow in question. 'What way?'

Dana shrugged as she helped herself to mini-spring rolls. 'Jack's feelings are important to you. Unless I'm completely wrong about the way you keep looking at him when he doesn't notice.'

Tara felt her cheeks grow warm, thought about denying it, then saw warmth in Dana's eyes and opted for honesty. 'You're not completely wrong.'

Dana grinned a familiar-looking grin. 'I hoped I wasn't.'

'It wasn't my idea, though.'

'I think that's the reason why my sisters all like you so much.'

Tara shook her head. 'The verdict's still undecided with Tess.'

Dana pursed her lips slightly, her eyes straying to where Tara had so recently looked. 'It's tough being the eldest. You have to be protective of everyone else. Jack moving away from us hurt Tess the most. It was like she'd failed him in some way—like it was her responsibility to be our mother when the real thing left.'

Tara nodded. 'That's understandable.'

They moved away from the table, finding seats beside the huge open fireplace that Rachel had filled with scented candles. Dana picked at things on her plate while Tara continued watching Jack and Tess. Jack was frowning now, looking away from Tess's face as often as possible.

'Is your family close, Tara?'

'Not really.' She glanced down at her plate. 'My parents are both gone and I only see my brother once in a blue moon.'

'I'm sorry. It must get lonely from time to time.'

'It's no big deal. But it's different from this.' Tara waved an arm towards the full room.

In every chair there was a Lewis of some form or another. Bill, the birthday boy, was surrounded by family of varying sizes: Tess's husband and Sam, Lauren tucked in close to her husband's side, Dana's daughter torturing the family Labrador, and Rachel, her husband and their four children. 'Christmas must be an expensive time of year.'

'Wouldn't have it any other way.' Dana grinned. 'There was never much time spent feeling lonely growing up, and I loved that.'

They were my family too. Sarah's words echoed in her ears and Tara tried to imagine how it would feel to be a part of so many people's lives. It must have been tough to let go of. For Tara, losing a family like this would be almost as unbearable a loss as the one she imagined she'd feel if she lost the man she loved. Yet another reason why she should be fighting the warmth she felt in her chest when Jack looked at her, when he reached out to brush her hair back from her face or held her hand in his.

Watching her own family as she grew up had hardly given her a firm belief in happily ever after. It was part of the reason she'd immersed herself so much in her fantasy worlds. They were safer, controllable, and people could have the happiness with each other that she herself had never witnessed or found. But then, she'd long since stopped looking—hadn't she?

She frowned down at her plate, moving food around it with the end of her fork. 'You were very lucky.'

Dana examined the top of her head for a moment, her voice soft when she spoke. 'Yeah, I know.'

'Why did you bring her?'

'What kind of question is that?' Jack kept his voice low as he faced off against his eldest sister. A sudden wave of protectiveness towards Tara formed again in his chest area. 'Anyone would think you didn't like her.'

'I don't know her well enough to like her or not like her.' Tess shook her head in frustration. 'I just think it's inappropriate of you to get involved with someone else while you're still not past the whole Sarah thing.'

'When it's all too obvious how crap I am at picking the right person to get involved with, you mean?' He swallowed a mouthful of coffee. 'I should just hold Tara at arm's length until I've proved I'm a decent guy again, should I?'

'You aren't holding her at arm's length now? Like you do with all of us?'

'What does that mean?'

Tess shook her head. 'Ever since you made changes to your life and realised the big mistake you'd made with Sarah you've been hurting. And don't think for one second we don't all know it. It's why you keep moving around so much. What do you think you're doing? Protecting us in some way? Well, maybe we'd like to have been there for you, Jack. And maybe we'd like to be there for you now. Stop shutting us all out and pretending you're fine when you're not.'

'I can look after myself, Tess.'

'No, you can't. What you'll do is close off, like you did last time.'

'I did not *close off.*' Jack took a breath to calm his temper. 'And I really wish you would stop taking everything I do so damned person- ally. I took time to myself, thought about what had happened, and sorted it out in my head. And I did it without you lot having the need to feel sorry for me all the time!'

Tess frowned at the low tone of his words. 'We're a *family*. We're supposed to be there for each other and you never gave us a chance to do that for you. You can't tell me that this fight with Sarah isn't threatening everything you've worked so hard for. Or that knowing that doesn't hurt some more.'

'So you think I should just let you lot all make me cups of sweet tea and hug me 'til she goes away? I'll fight this, Tess. I'll fight it and

I'll win. Because it's my life and she won't take it away from me—no matter what I did to her. She can claim to have been some sort of common-law wife all she wants, but she wasn't there while I did all the work.'

'I know that!' Tess looked around to make sure no one had noticed her raised tone. 'You've been carrying this damn guilt around for long enough now! You let her go, gave her a chance to find someone who loved her in a way you didn't—and that was a brave thing, Jack. I'm not saying you should give in without a fight now. But we have a right as your family to be there if you need us—just to talk, if that's all you need—and we can't do that if you do this whole macho male crap.'

'It's not crap. I can deal with this.'

'I'm not saying you can't.' She sighed. 'What I'm trying to say is, you have your hang-ups. Hell, Squirt, we all do. But you can't let your experiences with Sarah cloud the way you are with the rest of the world. You *are* defensive. Tara got that much right. But you're defensive because you're vulnerable. And probably a little scared—not that you'd admit it.'

Jack looked over at Tara for a moment. She turned her face towards him and smiled softly.

Instantly he felt some of the tension in his body relaxing. It was like turning his face towards the sun on a cold day. He smiled back, then looked back at his sister. 'Isn't everyone? She was right; you're right. I am defensive. Welcome to the modern world. There isn't anyone out there who isn't a little scared about getting made a fool of or falling for the wrong person.'

'Your timing on a new relationship sucks, though, you know that?'

He nodded slowly. 'Possibly, yes. But it's not like I went looking for her. I can't explain why, but even with all our joint hang-ups we just sort of fit—right now.'

Tess blinked slowly. 'She's that important already?'

God help him. 'Looks like.' He shrugged. 'I don't know why.'

She quirked an eyebrow. 'Don't you?'

'Maybe I have an idea.' He stared her straight in the eye. 'Maybe I'm not quite ready to talk to *you* about it yet. Of everyone in this family you're the one most likely to point out all the pitfalls—which balances out the optimists just fine, but isn't exactly encouragement for those of us who are pessimistic already.'

'Fine. I'll just stop caring, then, shall I?'

'Tess, for crying out loud!' He scowled down at her. 'I know that you care. I'm glad that you care. You're my sister, and I will love you for the rest of my life. But you need to let me take my own chances and live my own life. I'm big enough and—' he kept a straight face '—handsome enough to do that. When I need you I know you'll be there. That goes both ways.'

'Politely translated as, "Butt out, Tess"?'

'On this occasion. Yes.'

Tess looked up at him with sad eyes. She studied his face before nodding. 'I'll stay out of it, Jack. But you have to know I'm only concerned for you. We've just got you back, and I for one don't want you to disappear off hiding like some recluse for months on end again.'

'I won't.'

'Just take your time with Tara.' She reached out and squeezed his arm. 'If you care about her then you'll not test her by getting her involved in something you're not ready to make last. She's your first relationship since Sarah—first serious one—and more than likely that means it won't last.'

'Now you're concerned about Tara?'

'I don't know Tara. I know you. And if you end up breaking her heart you'll eat yourself up with guilt for a long time. I don't want to see that happen.'

CHAPTER NINE

As she made the final turn towards her own house Tara's eyes fell on the lines of a now familiar sports car. Her stomach cramped. The woman was like a dose of the flu. Just when you thought it was shaken off it came right back. Tara wondered idly whether a hit-man cost a lot of money.

Having spent the day in the city with Mags and Lizzie doing bridesmaid things, she had been in a buoyant mood, smiling and tingling with what could only be excitement about spending time with Jack. Doing whatever came to mind when she set eyes on him. Mags had even had a few suggestions.

She parked her car in front of her house and glared out of the side window. What had Sarah done? Waited until she'd left and then swooped in like some vulture? Cow.

Her fingers drummed on the steering wheel.

She could march on over to the house and demand to know what was going on. No, too much like a daytime soap opera. She could tiptoe up the steps and spy through the windows. Glancing down at her toes with a frown of concentration, she realised that her heels would be heard too easily on a wooden porch.

Her fingers drummed some more.

They had a relationship now, she guessed. Nothing written in stone, as Jack had once said, but there was definitely something going on. Something good too. Or at least the beginnings of it. Tara wasn't too stupid or too stubborn to admit that. And she couldn't deny how she felt when he was around.

But with another frown she also knew that it could still be easily broken. Just because they didn't spend every minute bickering with each other it didn't mean that they were on solid ground. But with the bickering down to a healthy, sexually charged flirtation, and the touching and kissing a much more open thing, they had crossed a line.

He hated Sarah's guts, for crying out loud! Tara felt that showed he had excellent taste. The woman irritated the hell out of *her*. So why would he even want to talk to her?

She drummed her fingers some more. *Men.*

The drumming continued for ten long minutes while Tara's mind argued with her gut. For some reason she felt—no, just *knew*—that there wasn't anything going on between Jack and the ever-present Sarah. 'You have nothing to worry about,' he'd told her. And, whether she was right or wrong, she believed him.

But that still didn't stop her from not being happy that Venom-Woman was there. Did the woman have any idea at all what she could do to her in print? Even now, the other Jack's ex was mentally being eaten by piranhas. *Ha.* Served her right.

Jack stared at the silhouette in the driver's seat. She'd been sitting still for an age now. What was with that? There must be one great song playing, or maybe she was talking to one of those crazy women she knew on her mobile. The workings of Tara's mind still remained both a mystery and a fascination.

Sarah's voice continued to echo around the empty room.

'I only want what's rightfully mine. What's owed to me.'

Jack took a breath. 'And you think that half of everything I've made over the last few years is rightfully yours?'

She was silent for a moment, then, 'You would never have been able to buy all those houses if you hadn't made money on the first one. The one we bought together.'

'The one you more than got your money back on.'

'I *invested* in you.'

He scowled at his own reflection in the glass. 'That's romantic.'

Sarah shook her head, a frown creasing her perfect features. 'It was you who changed. You weren't the man I got engaged to—the ambitious man, the man who was going places. Instead you turned into some kind of bloody labourer!'

'I'm happier doing this. If you'd loved me as much as you thought you did you'd have been happy that I was happy! I was just the one who had the guts to say it out loud.' Silence occupied the room for several moments. 'Touché.'

Her footsteps sounded on the floor, closer, her voice was low. 'You knew I was ambitious, Jack. That I'd made long-term plans. You knew I wanted to get married—we might even have had that family you wanted so badly. You took all that away the moment you started with these stupid projects of yours. This life—' the air at his shoulder moved as she waved a hand at the empty room '—really just isn't for me.' She laughed. 'And you knew that the moment you made the decision to start this up.'

'Water under the bridge, Sarah.' His jaw clenched and unclenched, his eyes still fixed on Tara's silhouette. Sarah was leaving out as much as she was putting into the re-hash of their past, and he knew it. 'I can't go back and change what happened. We weren't right. That's all. And I couldn't change that. What I give a damn about now is what I've worked for.' He turned to face her. 'So how much exactly is it going to take to get you to go away?'

He wanted to be in the car with Tara. Away from the past that didn't mean squat any more. He wanted to be warmed by easy bantering, challenged by her. He wanted it almost too much. Beyond levels of reasonable operational safety.

Tess's words echoed in his mind. *If you end up breaking her heart you'll eat yourself up with guilt for a long time.*

'Half, Jack. Like I've said before.'

Maybe he relied on Tara being there too much already. Even as he stood in the cold room with Sarah he wanted the warmth of being with Tara.

'You'll never get half.'

Where were they going with this thing anyway? It was something he knew he had to take some time to think about. At some point they'd have to move forward, wouldn't they? It was what normally happened in a relationship.

Good God, now he was thinking in terms of a *relationship*?

'I'll get it. More if I can. I've already wasted too much of my life on you. You owe me for that time.'

Marriage? Kids? All those things he'd accepted weren't for him after Sarah?

He swung round to face Sarah, surprised momentarily by the look of vindictiveness in her eyes. Clearing his vision with a shake of his head, he smiled coldly. 'You won't get it. I'll fight you all the way. You can take a small settlement now—call it the price I have to pay for past mistakes—and you can sign a letter waiving all further claims, or I'll fight you and you'll risk getting squat.'

She stared at him.

His blue eyes blinked slowly. 'Understand me, Sarah. I've had about enough of this. No more. It's done.'

'What will your little girlfriend think when you end up penniless, Jack? Will she support you both with her little stories? My, but you've changed if you're ready to have a woman support you until you're back on your feet.'

'Get out.' His eyes sparked as he threw the words down at her. 'If I didn't know I wasn't in love with you before, then I sure as hell know now.'

'I'll see you in court.'

She turned from the room, Jack's angry words following her. 'You're damn right you will.'

Tara got sick of sitting and obsessing in her car. Eventually. And she knew that being inside her house would lead to more obsessing. So she went for a walk instead. It would be therapeutic, in theory.

Her mind dug out the memories of his father's birthday party the night before, and her conversations with Dana and Rachel. Only Tess had really avoided her, though she had felt her eyes burning into the back of her skull for much of the night.

'It's great to see Jack so happy with someone new.'

'You're a brave woman, you know. He's not easy.'

Tara had smiled. 'You think?'

'But he's worth it.'

Tara had watched him tumble around with his nieces and nephews. She'd caught the subtle manly affection between father and son, the former a living example of how handsome Jack would still be as he got older. It was probably then she'd started to realise she was in love with him.

But it was only while standing alone, looking out on the water, that she was ready to face up to it. And by then, with Sarah's car still parked outside his house, Tara's heart was already starting to break. So much for being happy with the single life. It had taken Jack to show her what was possible by not being alone. By letting her guard down enough to let him into her life, her mind and her heart. Damn the man.

How long would it be before she was alone again?

*   *   *

Some time after the party their relationship started to change.

Jack couldn't quite put his finger on what it was, but he found himself staring at Tara a little more every day, trying to discover what it was. It was as if the spark had started to go out of her. He really needed to know why. He just wasn't sure he wanted to know the answer to the why.

His chest did a weird twisting thing when he first saw her in the bridesmaid dress. She was stunning. From the halo of hair that shone like pale gold in the candlelight to the almost serene smile she wore as she watched her friend taking her vows.

All through the service he couldn't take his eyes off her. Afterwards he couldn't remember anything from the event except what Tara had looked like, what she had worn, how she had turned her head or blinked with large eyes that filled with tears when the songs were sung. They might as well have been in an empty room.

'You're the dancing guy.'

The reception was a different matter. The crazy brigade were there *en masse*.

'The dancing guy?'

'From the bar that night.' Lizzie, the bride, was visiting tables after the meal. 'You swept Tara clean off her feet, if memory serves.'

He grinned at her choice of words. 'That would be me.'

An elegant creature facing him smiled knowingly. 'You've been quite the topic of conversation recently.'

'I can imagine.'

'I really don't think you can, actually.' The woman smiled seductively.

Jack suddenly felt threatened. She was scary. Even as she studied him he could feel the sensation of being measured for a roasting dish. He blinked at her.

'Oh, don't worry, honey.' She waved a hand at him. 'It's not your fault. It's just that men really have no idea what women actually talk about. It's easier for you all to believe we're still genuinely interested in recipes and knitting. Makes us less threatening.'

Not this one, it didn't.

'That's Laura.' Lizzie smiled sympathetically at him. 'You're safe while you're with Tara, but if you weren't...' she leaned closer to stage-whisper '...I'd advise you to run and not look back.'

Mags, his companion for the meal, smiled over at him. 'That's if you don't want to be caught, you understand.'

'And there's many the one that does.'

They all glanced across at Laura. She shrugged. 'When you've got it, you've got it.'

Jack smiled a slow smile. 'I have a friend, Adam, you should meet him some time. I think you guys would love each other. You're very similar.'

'Has he a nice car?'

He nodded. 'Just got a Porsche.'

Her card magically appeared on the table. 'Get him to give me a call.'

Tara appeared at the scary woman's shoulder, her smile warm. 'Hey, all. What have I missed?'

'We were all just meeting Jack.' Lizzie returned her smile. 'He's yum.'

Yum? He grimaced at the description. 'Yep, that's me. I'm just the yummiest.' He shook his shoulders and blew Tara a kiss. 'Don't you think, babe?'

She laughed. 'Oh, yeah. Candy-coated Jack; that's you all over.'

Though it had to be said he *was* fairly delicious in a suit. Nearly every woman in the room had noticed that. Well, everyone except the bride.

Music started up in the background.

Lizzie looked around the table. 'Trust Tara to end up bringing someone as good-looking as the guys she writes about in her books.'

'It's like that one you were telling us about recently—you know, the one you based on some labourer you kept seeing.'

Tara's face froze in a weak smile. 'That was ages ago, Laura.'

She moved towards Jack, glancing back at her friend's face with a 'don't you dare' look.

But he'd already swallowed the bait. 'Which one was that?'

Laura continued, despite Tara giving her the absolute best evil eye. 'Oh, sweetie, you know…' She sipped some champagne. 'That guy you watched for weeks on end. Didn't you lust after him big-style and then let your filthy imagination fill in the rest? I guess there is a little real life in everything that gets written, right?'

'Lusted after big-style? Really?' He glanced up at Tara from the corner of his eye. 'Was he good-looking, this guy?'

Tara avoided his eyes and smiled sickly-sweetly at Laura. 'Oh, just average. Nothing special.'

'But you lusted after him enough to do some *fantasising*?'

Somehow he managed to smile and make it seem as if he was teasing, while his gut twisted and he felt his hand clench into a ball under the table. Damn it. He was jealous. He couldn't ever remember having felt that before. It wasn't a pleasant sensation. In fact, he'd rather have had teeth pulled.

Her eyes swept back to lock with his. 'Fantasising is what gets me all of my stories, Jack. Surely that makes sense?'

Not if she was fantasising about someone who wasn't him!

'Oh, this guy really had her hot. Trust me. She locked herself away and wrote for ages.'

Tara wanted to slap Laura silly. She raised an eyebrow, as if to question whether she actually knew what she was talking about. Or, more importantly, *who* she was talking about.

The twinkling in Laura's eyes told her she knew perfectly well. Tara tapped Jack on the shoulder. 'Maybe we should dance now.'

'Good idea.' He smiled at everyone before turning to grasp Tara's hand in an almost vice-like grip.

'Jack, you're hurting my hand.' Tara teetered along behind him in her ridiculously high heels. 'Jack, slow down, would you? My hand?'

He turned to face her, blinked, then looked down at her hand in his. His hold eased and he rubbed his thumb across her knuckles before pulling her into his arms to sway with the music. 'About this guy...'

'What about him?'

'Do you still see him?'

'From time to time.' She avoided his stare.

'You still lust after him?'

Oh, yes. 'It's not what you think.'

'Then explain it.'

His tone caught her attention. Glancing back at his face, she was shocked by the anger she saw there. She let the wheels turn in her mind. 'You're *jealous*?'

'If you're running around getting hot under the collar for some other guy while spending time with me?' He frowned. 'Hell, yes.'

She shook her head slowly. 'It's really not what you think.'

His frown deepened as she smiled a slow smile up at him, her eyes glowing. She *liked* that he was jealous? What the hell was it with women? It was as if he'd just scored points or something.

'The guy in question—'

He changed his mind. Guys could do that too. 'I don't need to hear it.'

'I think you do.'

'Maybe it's something you need to do, Tara.'

'What?' She frowned in confusion.

'Maybe in order to write about some amazing hero-type you have to fixate on someone from a distance to—' he searched for the right words '—get your juices flowing.'

Her eyes widened in shock.

'Creatively speaking.'

'I do no such damn thing!'

'Then where does this guy come into it?'

'I have never lusted after someone from a distance like that before. It was a one-off.' She let the words come out in a rush. Sometimes confessions were easier if they were spoken quickly.

Jack held her a little tighter, his lips pursing. 'So maybe that means something, then.'

'Maybe.'

He took a deep breath and looked past her as he spoke. 'Everything happens for a reason, doesn't it? Maybe you should just see if there's anything in it.' He looked into her eyes, his expression unreadable. 'Fate, or something like that.'

She pressed her body to his and tilted her head to look up at him. 'If fate was going to enter into it, then it probably kicked in when I went and gave my hero the same name as the guy I'd been watching.'

It took several long seconds for the meaning of her words to hit his brain. Tara watched as realisation widened his eyes.

'It was *me*?'

She nodded.

'You were *watching* me?'

She felt the warmth start to grow up over her neck. 'It was an unintentional thing. Really.'

'You were lusting after me from a distance?'

The warmth spread up over her jawline. She cleared her throat. 'You were out there every day, working on that house right outside my window while I was trying to write. It just kind of happened…'

The wheels continued to turn. 'Now, let me just get this straight here. The Jack Lewis in your book is based on *me*?'

She nodded again.

'So when I first told you what my name was—'

'I took a freak attack.'

'I remember.'

'I thought someone had told you.'

'You thought you'd been caught out perving through your window.'

'Well, yes.' Her face felt as if it was on fire. 'Something like that. It was just too freaky.'

'I can see how it would have been.'

'It still is a little.' She tried to justify her freak attack. 'I mean, I could have picked thousands of name combinations—millions.'

'And you chose Jack Lewis?'

'Yes.'

'You must have heard my name somewhere.'

'I'm not senile. My memory works just fine.' She glared at him. 'I'd have remembered what your name was if someone had told me.'

He studied her face, looking for any sign of deception. Then he looked around the room again, giving himself time to process this new information. He sighed as he thought. This was too weird. Even for Tara.

'Say something. I'm dying over here.'

'What do you want me to say?'

'Like *I* know? Something. Find me an explanation for it. I sure as hell can't. And believe me, I've tried.'

He looked down at her again. 'So all that time you were fighting me off so hard—that time when you hit me with the soup—you were *already* attracted to me?'

'Not to you.' She frowned at his look of disbelief. 'To the fantasy you. The one I'd watched from a distance and formed a character around. I didn't know *you*.'

Jack asked the million-dollar question. 'And how does the real me measure up?'

Now she was onto male ego territory. She had worried for what seemed like an age about that exact same question. If he'd fallen short of the fantasy image she'd have been more than disappointed—and maybe, with the benefit of hindsight, that was the reason she'd fought him off so hard. It would have been simpler to live with the fantasy than to be disappointed by the reality. Because if that had happened she'd have killed the attraction to both Jacks at the same time.

'You're more than him.' The confession put her out on that limb further than she'd ever planned on going. And yet there was still a bigger confession she could have made about her feelings. But she held it back—held it to her like a protective covering. If she could just manage not to say the words out loud, then if he rejected her she would have retained her dignity at least. 'You're real.'

'I live up to the fantasy you created?'

And then some. She did what he'd wanted her to do since nearly the beginning and spoke the thought aloud as it appeared in her head. 'And then some.'

He swayed their bodies to the music as her words swung round and round in circles in his brain. Telling him that had cost her. The fact that she'd lusted after him from a distance was weird enough. He'd never been stalked before. His mind played with different explanations,

'Was this all some big research thing for you, then?'

'No!'

His chest rose and fell in huge breaths as he kept reminding himself to complete the essential function. His head was starting to hurt.

'Curiosity, maybe?'

'No.'

'You had no intention of trying to live out your fantasies?'

'No. It never entered my head. But then you were there.' She smiled weakly. 'And you just wouldn't quit.'

He finally looked down at her, his eyes searching her face, roving over her hair, before he looked into her eyes. She blinked up at him, long lashes brushing against her flushed cheeks. She tried to will him to see the sincerity in her eyes. If she was going to lose him she didn't want it to be over this.

His mind made a startling discovery. 'You kept fighting me off because you were scared?'

'Yes.'

He continued to figure it out. 'Of my being exactly the man you had fantasised about?'

'Yes.' The word came out on a sigh.

'Your hero?'

She smiled a soft smile. 'Something like that.'

'That's a big responsibility.'

'If I'd told you at the start you'd have run a mile.'

'I thought you wanted me to stay away.'

'I guess a part of me didn't.'

He continued to stare at her, still swaying their bodies with the music. 'If you'd told me it would have completely freaked me out.'

'Like it did with me to begin with.'

The music wrapped around them like a blanket as it changed smoothly from one song to another. Jack continued to stare down at her.

'Tara?'

She smiled again. 'Yes?'

He searched her eyes, his breath held painfully in his chest.

With a small frown he continued to figure it all out. After all, he wasn't dumb. Many things he might be, and a great many not good, but he wasn't dumb.

'Are you by any chance in love with me?'

Her heart forgot to beat for a couple of seconds, then sped up to compensate.

'Would it matter to you if I was?'

'That's not an answer.'

'Neither's that.'

'I'm no hero.'

She glanced down to where their bodies touched. 'You don't have to be, Jack. You do just fine as you.' She glanced up with a slight twinkle in her eyes. 'Flaws and all.'

Flaws and all. Fear of emotional attachment and all. Baggage from previous relationships and all. Tara Devlin was searching for a hero. She filled her life with fantasy ones to make up for the lack of them in real life. It suddenly all made perfect sense.

As did the reality of his own life. What sort of a hero was he, exactly? A pretty damn poor one.

If you end up breaking her heart you'll eat yourself up with guilt for a long time.

Maybe it was better to take the punishment himself than take the chance of her realising he fell way short of being her hero. Because he couldn't make a guarantee to her, could he? Couldn't look her in the eye and tell her that he wouldn't hurt her one day, make her waste years of her life waiting for him to make a commitment.

As he'd done with Sarah.

He'd believed he was in love with Sarah once. Believed that they had a life ahead of them together. Believed it enough to propose. And he'd been wrong.

This time was different. This time he knew he loved Tara—loved her enough to not want to let her down. To not take a chance on being less than she deserved or needed. To not wait around and see the light in her eyes die as it had started to these last few days.

Then there was the whole financial thing to add to it. What kind of man would he be if he stepped into something serious with her without a penny to his name? He searched for more excuses to let her go. More reasons to justify that it was the chivalrous thing to do. But it all came down to one thing.

He didn't trust himself to love her.

'Say something.'

'I can't.'

'I know this is all too weird.' He was still standing there, and her fragile heart began to hope a little.

'No.' He forced himself to keep eye contact. 'It's all too much.'

She felt her throat close as he stared at her with a completely blank expression.

'I'm sorry, Tara.'

Her heart hit her feet with a loud thud. So that was that. She managed to nod and not cry in front of him, even though it felt as if someone had just crushed her chest and broken every rib. 'I understand.'

He watched her turn her face from him, hiding her expressive eyes. 'I've never met anyone like you.'

'It's okay, Jack.'

'But this is just too much for me right now.'

She looked back at him with a smile. 'It's okay—really.'

'I hope that guy you wrote about is better than me, I really do.'

A nod as she pulled free from his arms. 'He will be. Don't worry.' She looked up at his face and memorised everything she could about the moment she'd had her heart broken for the first time,

'I'll see you around, Jack Lewis.'

He watched as she walked off the dance floor. Followed her movements as she weaved through tables to an exit. And then she was gone.

People danced around him, their bodies occasionally nudging his. He must have stood still for a full five minutes before he thought to move.

*   *   *

Mags studied Tara's pale face over the edge of her oversized coffee mug. She took in her almost translucent skin, the dark circles and the dull light in her eyes.

'You look like hell.'

'I love you too, Mags.'

'Well, you do.'

'I have the flu. It's a prerequisite to look like hell.'

Mags let out a small grunt of disbelief. 'The flu? Right—that'll be what it is. Nothing to do with the fact that for the first time in your life you've managed to fall in love—and, boy, have you fallen.'

Tara glared at her friend from her foetal position on Mags's large family sofa. 'And you had absolutely nothing to do with it, did you? You didn't encourage me to do the whole—' she made speech marks in the air with her fingers '—"take a chance on love" thing, did you?'

'I had no idea that you'd fall this hard, and if you'd ever just come out and tell me what horrible thing he did to break your heart then I could drive right over and kick him in the shins for you.' She smiled. 'Granted, I'd need a stepladder to reach them.'

Tara thought about smiling at the statement but just couldn't seem to summon the energy. She'd had no idea that being in love could feel so absolutely awful. In fact, she wondered how her editor had ever bought anything she'd written, when her experience of the emotion was so completely lacking.

Mags had reliably helped her through the first symptoms of the broken heart/flu combination with dry toast, fleecy blankets and a rationed amount of sympathy.

'So, are you going to tell me?'

Tara sighed, her eyes focused on the colourful children's characters singing on the TV screen. 'Tell you what?'

'Why you're so miserable you're making yourself physically sick?'

'I have the flu!'

'Right. Sure you do.'

Tara sniffed, tears forming at the back of her stinging eyes. 'A girl can't even have a perfectly reasonable germ now without getting grief. How about I make up a reason anyway just to keep you quiet? Will that do?'

'Is there a grain of truth in it?'

'Why don't you decide for yourself?'

'Ooh—moody, aren't we?'

She groaned and hid her face underneath the blanket, her voice muffled. 'Can't you just leave me be?'

'Nope.' Mags smiled at the hand peeking over the edge of the blanket. 'It's my house, and if I'm not here to hold your hair back while you're throwing up then all my parenting skill certificates will be revoked.'

There was a sniff, then silence. Mags sipped more coffee and waited for nearly a full minute. 'Still alive in there?'

Silence.

'Okay. I can wait.' She sipped again. 'Let me know when you're ready to talk.'

Tara's nose reappeared at the blanket-edge. Her voice was still muffled. 'I'm in love with Jack.'

'I got that bit, sweetie.'

The blanket lowered further. '*No*. I mean, really head over heels, will-probably-never-recover-for-the-rest-of-my-days *in love*.'

Mags nodded. 'Uh-huh.'

Tara frowned. 'How did that happen, exactly?'

'Well, my guess would be you took one look at that hunk of gorgeous male and your libido kicked in. That's often the start of it, you know.'

Tara continued frowning. 'But that's not the way it's supposed to happen!'

'No? It's worked for plenty of people before you.'

'What happened to the wooing?'

'The wooing?'

'Yes.' She folded the blanket neatly beneath her chin. 'You know—the part where he woos me, the courting part.'

'And this big arguing thing you two have going on isn't wooing? You know, in a basic form?'

Her lips formed a delicate pout. 'I don't know. Maybe. I guess.'

Mags smiled. 'I've always adored that decisive side to your nature.'

'I don't want to be in love with him.'

'I know.'

'I don't want to be in love with anyone.'

'Of course you don't.' She tutted. '*Men*, right?'

'It's not like I want to be alone for ever—'

'Of course you don't. No one does.'

'But I just thought it would be someone—I don't know—less—'

'Heartbreaker material?'

'Yes, exactly that.' She managed a smile. 'Just someone more—you know—'

'Two point four kids and a Labrador material?'

'Yes! You see, I knew you'd know.'

'Because that's what will sustain a relationship through the years.'

'Security, reliability, mutual understanding.'

Mags nodded her head. 'All very important things.'

They both watched the TV.

Mags blinked a few times. 'Some passion would be nice, you know, on cold winter nights…'

'I guess so.'

'Otherwise the whole making of the two point four kids would be a bit boring. After all, it can take a few attempts—several nights of practising to get it right. And if you're going to practise it may as well be…well, you know *good*. Like Laura so wisely said. The Dalai Lama has nothing on her, you know.'

Tara blushed a fiery red. 'Well, she actually does make some sense.'

Mags raised an eyebrow. 'Unless, of course, you're telling me that Jack isn't any good at—'

One finger waved a warning in the air. 'Don't go there.'

A wicked grin appeared. 'Yeah, thought as much. He didn't look like the kind of man who'd need an instructional video.'

'Mags!'

'Okay.' She held her hand up. 'I'll stop. But you do have to admit it's a point in his favour. Would he be a good father?'

Tara closed her eyes. Memories of Jack with Sam and his other nieces and nephews played across the backs of her eyelids like pictures on a cinema screen. She thought about the huge family any child of his would automatically inherit, about how four little girls had helped raise their younger brother between them. About the bond they all shared. Would he make a good father? He'd be the best.

Looking at Mags with tear-filled eyes, she nodded her head, biting on her bottom lip.

'So from what I know—' Mags began to count on her fingers, purposely avoiding hugging Tara '—he's gorgeous to look at, has a sense of humour, he challenges and encourages you, he's good with children and makes a good living. How am I doing here? Any lies so far?'

Tara shook her head.

'Right.' She held up a thumb. 'And that's before we hit the whole horizontal mambo thing…'

The smile was a little watery. 'Okay, so I have fairly good taste in men.'

'Pretty much.'

Tara groaned as a wave of nausea hit her stomach. 'It's just a shame he wants nothing more to do with me, really, isn't it?'

Mags stared in shock at her statement, then watched in amazement as her together friend burst into tears. 'What the hell happened?'

'I think—he figured out—I'm in—love—with him.' Tara choked out the words.

'And he dumped you?'

'Only—when he realised—I was a—stalker.'

'What?'

'He said—it was—just too much for him.'

'Tara, I haven't the faintest notion what you're talking about.'

She sniffed loudly. 'And I'm a liar. A big fat liar.'

Mags shook her head. 'No, you're not. Well, at least if I knew what you were talking about I'd tell you you're not. Why do you think you're a liar?'

'Because…' She blew her nose into a tissue. 'I've been writing romance all this time and I never knew that being in love hurt so bloody much.'

And then she threw up.

CHAPTER TEN

'YOU look awful. You know that, don't you, Jack?'

Jack raised an eyebrow as he looked down. 'Who? Me? You must be mistaking me for someone else. I always look great, even first thing in the morning. It's a gift.'

'Yeah, sure you do. That's just typical of you, isn't it?' Tess poked him in the stomach. 'Far be it from you to admit in public to being unhappy. Lightning might hit you, right?'

'It might.' His chin dropped. 'You can never be too careful.'

Tess took a slow breath. 'I'm guessing Tara.'

'Don't start.'

'I've butted out for ages now.'

'And your prize is in the mail.'

Her perceptive eyes studied the top of his head intently. 'Did you two have some kind of falling out?'

'I think...' he continued staring downwards '...that would be an understatement. I'm not seeing her any more.' He glanced up to meet her eyes. 'Which I'm sure you'll be chuffed to bits to hear.'

'What happened?'

'It doesn't matter.'

'When you look this miserable I think it does.'

Jack looked down to the ground again and thought about arguing it out with his elder sister. What the hell? 'Yes, maybe it does. But it doesn't really make any difference now. I screwed up. Again.'

'You love her?'

'Doesn't matter if I do.'

Tess laughed out loud. 'Oh, of course it doesn't. No big deal, right? That kind of thing happens to you every day.'

He looked at her with anger in his eyes. 'You don't even like her. *You* thought it was bad timing for a relationship with someone new.' He laughed slightly. 'And as it turns out you were right.'

Tess blinked up at him with wide eyes. 'I never said I didn't like her, Jack. I like her just fine if *you're* happy—and right now, without her, you're obviously not. I guess there *is* no right or wrong time to fall in love.'

Jack shrugged his shoulders and looked out at the rest of the packed room. Yet another birthday. He was beginning to think they should have a single family birthday, like Christmas, when they could all just exchange presents at once. It would be a lot simpler—fewer dates to remember and he wouldn't have to answer to the Spanish Inquisition every time he glanced sideways.

Tess waited for a few moments. 'She dump you?'

His jaw clenched. 'No, actually. I ended it.'

'While you're in love with her? That makes sense.'

'I didn't say I was in love with her.'

'Yeah, but you are, though.'

'Tess, I just didn't think I was the guy for her. She's looking for a hero, and right now I'm not even close to being a hero's sidekick. With or without tights.'

Tess quirked an eyebrow. 'Can you stop being flippant for just one minute? You really can overdo it sometimes.' She thought for a moment. 'This isn't because of the Sarah thing, is it?'

He waited, thought a little, then answered. 'Maybe.'

'So not only does she get to punish you for ever, she also gets to make sure you're never given a chance at being happy? You really do have a guilt problem, you know.'

His eyes rolled skyward. This was just great. It never rained…

'Are you ever going to get off my case, Tess?' He glared at her. 'Because this is getting pretty damn tiring now.'

'Tough.'

'You don't have to play Mother with me any more, you know. I'm all grown up.'

'Then act like it. Don't let your past dictate your future, Jack.'

'And what would you have had me do?' he snapped, his already frayed patience tested to beyond its capabilities. 'Have Tara support me after Sarah had taken everything away? That would have been a great start, don't you think?'

Tess looked stunned. 'You split up with Tara because you think she'll not love you if you're not completely financially independent?'

'No! Aw, hell, Tess. Partly—maybe.'

She looked up at him for several long silent seconds. 'You prat.'

Jack threw his hands in the air. 'Great—just great.' He turned on his heel and marched towards the kitchen. 'I really need this right now.'

'It's not my fault you're emotionally constipated.'

'Emotionally constipated?' He swung round to face her again when they reached the kitchen. 'I am not emotionally constipated!'

'The hell you're not.' She moved across until her back was against the counter-top, then stretched her arms behind her so she could bounce up onto its smooth surface. 'You've been having problems with your emotions ever since Sarah. You think you're some kind of infallible being, someone who should never be able to make a mistake. Well, tough. You're human.' She shrugged. 'Accept it.'

Jack looked like a pot of water about to boil over. 'You have absolutely no idea what you're talking about. I've done fine on my own. Tess, I just thought I didn't need to mess up years of someone else's life!'

'Oh, who are you kidding? I know you still feel guilty that you made a mistake with Sarah. But she wasn't the one for you. You weren't the one for her. That's all it was. It happens. It took guts to face up to that, and one of you damn well had to.'

His eyes narrowed.

She dropped her voice slightly. 'You must also think I don't know what you've been doing with all these houses all this time.'

His chest heaved up and down.

Tess's eyes softened. 'Well, newsflash, Squirt. I know rightly. You've been making *homes*. Homes for families. And deep down I think *you* know that in the back of your mind you've always been making them for your own family. The one you want so bad you can't admit it. Because if you did then you'd have to face up to how lonely you actually are.'

Jack's boiling blood returned to a simmer, then cooled. He stared across at his sister. 'You think that's what I've been doing?'

'Yes, I do.'

He clenched his jaw, unclenched it, then clenched it again. 'If you were so sure that was what I was doing, then why were you so against my relationship with Tara?'

'I was against the idea of you falling for someone because they were just *there*. Because you wanted to commit to someone even if it wasn't the right one. That would have been an even bigger mistake than the one you made last time.'

'That's not the reason I love her, Tess.'

Tess nodded. 'I'm getting that now. You wouldn't be this miserable if she meant nothing. Does *she* love you?'

He thought about how her eyes would soften when she looked at him, how she would tease him out of a mood, with the touch of her hand on his. Then he thought about the pain in her eyes when he'd last seen her. When he'd told her it was too much for him.

'I think maybe she does.' Though God alone knew why.

Tess smiled. 'Can you imagine yourself being remotely happy without her? Or, on the flipside, see yourself in fifty years' time *with* her, married with half a dozen mini Jack and Taras? That's usually the test.'

His shoulders slumped as he sighed. 'I'm already bloody miserable without her, and it's only been a week. And as for the second part— it has occurred to me that it might not be too bad, yes.'

'Well, then.' She swung her legs back and forth. 'I still think you're a prat. If she loves you and you love her, and you can see yourself married with half a dozen kids, then you're a prat for letting her get away. And even if I didn't like her it shouldn't have made a bit of difference to you. I never realised you were such a big fat chicken.'

Jack stared at her incredulously, then shook his head. 'I don't believe you're pointing all this out now. After the fact.'

Tess shrugged. 'You wouldn't have listened any earlier.'

He glanced down at his feet, then looked back into her eyes. 'Okay, I'll give you that. But don't worry. I'm planning on fixing it. I've been planning on fixing it ever since I realised how bad I've screwed up this time. It just took a day or two for me to realise what a bloody idiot I was being.'

'You're male. It comes with the territory.' She narrowed her eyes as another thought occurred. 'Do you have a plan for the Sarah thing too?'

A smile twitched the corners of his mouth. 'Dana came up with a plan on that one.'

'Oh, really?'

'Yep. Apparently you and I aren't the only ones with brains in the family.' The smile appeared. 'She wanted to join Donovan & Lewis as an interior designer, so she offered to buy into the company. I went one better and sold her my half. So I'm an employee now.'

'You're giving up your business?'

'I'm not giving it up. It's still there, and I still run it with Adam and Dana. I just don't do it on paper. It would only be worth a lot of money to me if we ever decided to sell, and we have no intention of doing that.' His smile softened in reassurance. 'I'm still doing what I love and I have one hell of a good salary. You should see my bonus scheme.'

Tess frowned. 'But Sarah will still come after half of the money from the sale, won't she?'

'Yep.' Jack grinned. 'I posted off her cheque for fifty euros yesterday.'

There was a moment of silence and then Tess roared with laughter. 'Clever. Very clever.'

'That sister of ours is devious. Poor Adam. Office life is about to get interesting, I'd say.'

They both smiled across the room and then silence fell again. Jack looked towards the doorway, and the sounds of their family beyond filtering through, but Tess was wise enough to know his mind was further away. 'So how are you going to convince Tara?'

He grimaced. 'I don't quite know yet.'

She thought for a moment. 'First you better start praying you can. Broken-hearted women can be tough to win round.'

His gut twisted. The thought of having broken her heart broke his too. That was being in love, wasn't it?

Tess smiled. 'And how exactly do you plan on proposing to her if you can't say the three little words to her face?'

He looked away from her, his voice tense. 'I'll say them.'

Tess grinned. 'You'll have to.'

'I will.' His jaw clenched on the words as his voice dropped. 'If I can find her.'

His sister raised an eyebrow. 'If that's your only problem, then I can help out there.'

Jack leaned his head back and looked up at the sign above the door. The rain washed down over his face and into the neckline of his sweater. This had to be just about the single worst idea he'd ever had.

He took a deep breath and walked into the hotel foyer. Shaking his head to dislodge the water that had spiked his hair ridiculously, he turned his killer smile on the receptionist. 'Hi, there, can you direct me to the writers' workshop?'

There were *millions* of them.

Wall to wall women, in varying shapes, sizes and ages. It was a nightmare. All he needed to complete the picture was to be stark naked. From the looks the women at the doorway gave him he might as well have been.

His palms were damp, so he shoved them in the pockets of his trousers. He thought about jingling the coins he found there, and removed his hands again for fear of looking like a pervert. He tried folding his arms across his chest.

To hell with it. He smiled broadly at the women looking at him, and winked when one of them smiled back. *If in doubt, brazen it out.*

'Ladies.'

'I swear, Mary, these evenings just get better and better.'

'Do you write historical adventure-slash-romance, young man?' The woman highlighted the slash with a swipe of her hand in mid-air.

'No, I can't say I do.' He continued smiling, trying his best to make eye contact. 'But I believe in romance, if that's any help.'

'Do you help with research?' one woman asked with a quirk of her eyebrow. 'You'd make a fortune at it.'

Jack laughed. 'I'll keep that in mind as a career move.'

The space around him seemed to be getting smaller.

'Is it someone's birthday?'

There was jostling in the crowd. '*Ooh*, is he a stripogram?'

'Excuse me.' A high-pitched voice sounded from the sea of faces. 'Excuse me—let me through, dears.' The crowd parted enough to let an elderly woman through. Her head wasn't much above Jack's waist level, and she squinted up at him with bespectacled eyes. 'You're large, aren't you?'

Jack managed not to choke—just. 'I've been told that.'

'Are you in the wrong place?'

An escape clause. He could just do this some other way. A more private, less surrounded-by-women way.

The phrase 'man or mouse' hit his mind. Then he thought about seeing Tara again and his smile reached right up into his eyes. 'No. I'm not in the wrong place.'

'This is the South East Writers' Workshop with special guest Tara Devlin. The emphasis is on writing romance this evening.'

'Yes, it is.' Jack nodded at the young woman on his left.

The small woman continued squinting up at him. 'Are you trying to improve your courting skills?'

The woman to his right nudged her friend in the ribs. 'I don't think he looks like the kind of man who would have a problem with that.'

'So what are you doing here?'

Jack leaned down slightly so that he could lower his voice. 'I'm trying to surprise someone.'

The woman on his left snorted. 'If you were planning on going ''boo'' you should probably realise you stand out a little in this crowd.'

A voice piped up. 'I have a place I could hide him.'

Tara smiled at the crowd of women who applauded when she was introduced. It seemed like a lifetime since she had last talked to a writers' group.

As she sat down at the head of the room she allowed her eyes to scan the sea of faces, stopping every now and again to make eye contact and smile. She was halfway round when her eyes had to move upwards to look into a blue her heart knew so well.

She gasped, then glanced at the women beside her as they talked to the audience. Looking back at him, she frowned, then raised her eyebrows in question.

Jack smiled back at her.

She frowned again, then jerked her head towards the door, indicating he should leave.

He in turn raised his eyebrows and shrugged, with a 'don't understand' motion.

I'm going to kill him. Tara smiled sweetly at the woman making introductions.

'And we'd just like to take this opportunity to thank Tara for providing three signed copies of *Indiscretion* for our monthly raffle.'

There was more applause. Tara looked back to find Jack joining in. She glared at him as he stretched his clapping hands in her direction. Her eyes widened in disbelief.

'So, without any further delay, ladies—Tara Devlin.'

Tara plastered a smile onto her face as the applause continued. For twenty-three seconds. She knew because she was counting at the time.

The floor was opened to questions.

'I was wondering where your ideas for stories come from?'

With a quick glance at Jack, that saw him leaning back with folded arms to listen, Tara smiled. 'Sometimes it's a film I don't like the ending of, or a place that inspires me. It can be a dozen different things, but ultimately it comes down to the characters and their relationship. How their personalities unfold as the story progresses is the important part.'

'Do you ever base anything you write on real-life experiences?'

Jack's eyebrow rose. He leaned forward to hear better.

'I think you can't write without putting some of your own personal experiences and emotions into the words.' Tara's teeth clenched as she continued. 'But, apart from falling a little in love with all my *fictional* heroes, I can honestly say the stories are not reflective of my own love-life.'

Jack's voice sounded in a small second of silence between questions. 'Do you still believe in happily ever after?'

Her eyes narrowed. 'I believe it's possible. For *some* people.' She forced her head to move, forced a smile in place. Maybe if she ignored him he would go away. *Take the hint.*

'I was wondering if you think that the hero types in your stories exist in real life?'

Her heart twisted painfully at the question. It was a blinder. *Did* she still think that her hero existed? Composing herself, she opted for a safe answer, avoiding Jack's steady gaze. 'I think there are heroes out there, yes.'

'Where do we find them?' piped a voice from the crowd.

'Believe me, I've looked!'

There was a wave of laughter.

Tara searched for an answer. She cleared her throat and the woman beside her held up a hand for silence. 'Ladies. Let Tara answer.'

'I reckon there's a potential hero at the back of the room here,' someone interrupted.

Oh, dear Lord. This just wasn't happening. Tara hid her eyes momentarily behind the hand rubbing at her temples.

'Is he single?'

Tara peeked from behind her hand in time to see Jack turn his most potent smile on the lady who had asked the question.

'That's a complicated question at the minute. But feel free to ask me again in about half an hour.'

Tara set her hand down on the table. What did he mean by that? Her eyes were drawn to a tiny woman who stood up to declare, 'This young man is here to surprise a lucky girl he hasn't seen in a while.'

There were smiles and a few giggles. 'Surprise her with what, exactly, Edith?'

'Well, why don't you ask him?'

All eyes moved in Jack's direction. Women turned in their seats to see better. Jack seemed to hesitate for a moment, but, being Jack, he recovered quickly and managed to flirt with half the room in the process. Tara shook her head. The man had more gall than any one person deserved. Even one who looked as good as he did.

Her heart played to an erratic beat as she continued to stare at him. It seemed like for ever since she'd last allowed her eyes the luxury of just roving over him. Damn him for looking so good. Damn him to hell and back for making her love him, even when he'd already broken her heart.

He held a hand up. 'No, really, ladies. Why don't we let Miss Devlin answer her question first? I for one would love to hear the answer.'

Tara blinked at him. 'What question?'

'The issue of the existence of heroes?' This smile was aimed directly at her, a softer, gentler smile that had her heart turning over in her chest. 'Do you think they're out there?'

The women all looked back at her.

She stared at him for a long moment before allowing her eyes to move back across the sea of faces. 'I think they're out there *somewhere*.'

'Where?' the owner of the original question asked, and the room seemed to go still.

Tara moved her head slightly to look directly at the woman. 'Everywhere, I think. If we just look for them.'

'You mean like firemen and rescue workers?'

She smiled. 'Well, they fit automatically. I guess I mean the ones we overlook—your everyday hero.'

'What's an everyday hero?'

Without conscious thought her eyes moved back to lock with Jack's. 'A man whose strength lies in knowing his own weaknesses. The kind of man who can open himself to his feelings and not see that as a failing. Someone who's brave enough to take a few chances. I think that's pretty heroic.'

Jack held her steady gaze.

Tara swallowed to loosen the tightness in her throat. 'It's all down to personal interpretation, but I guess every woman who falls in love sees her guy as her hero.'

The air crackled in the distance between them before Tara lowered her eyes to stare at the table top in front of her. She twined her fingers together and blinked hard, realising just how much she'd given away with her softly spoken words—as much about how deep her own feelings ran as anything else. Maybe a neon-flashing banner would have had a touch more subtlety.

The room stayed silent for several long moments, then the tiny woman pointed at Jack. 'You came to see *her*, didn't you?'

Jack smiled slowly. 'Yes.'

'Why here?'

Tara's eyes raised slightly to look at his face as he answered. She watched as a small flush touched his throat above the line of his plain black sweater.

He shrugged. 'It seemed like a good idea at the time. A writers' workshop discussing romance seemed like a romantic kind of place to tell her I'm in love with her.'

There was a collective sigh and all eyes turned to Tara's shocked face. Jack grinned while Tara gaped. 'And I think that's the quietest she's been since I've met her.'

Tara's stubborn streak kicked in. She raised her chin and an eyebrow simultaneously. 'What makes you think for one second I'm interested in hearing that?'

He continued to smile, recognising her defensive tactics. After all, he now knew them nearly as well as he knew his own. He figured he deserved to be given a hard time after the screwup he'd made. However, a little help from the troops could do no harm. 'Ladies, what do you think?'

His newly formed fan club jumped to his defence. 'Well, he *is* gorgeous.'

'I like his smile; it's roguish.'

'And it *is* a very romantic thing he's doing...'

Tara shook her head. 'You still don't get it, do you?'

Jack stood and edged his way out of the women as he tried to get closer to her. 'I thought you could maybe marry me. Because you maybe like me a little bit. Or because maybe you've been as miserable without me as I've been with-out you.'

He stopped in front of the small platform her table was standing on, shrugging his shoulders again. 'Or you could maybe say yes because you love me?'

The room held its breath.

Tara looked round at all the expectant faces, then, very slowly, her eyes returned to Jack's. 'Even now you can't just come and see me and tell me how you feel, can you, Jack? Simple words. You can't do that, can you?'

He frowned at her.

'You really just can't.' She smiled sadly. 'You'd rather hide behind a room full of people you don't know and rely on that ridiculous charm of yours to get you out of some serious talking.'

'As opposed to how well *you* handle your emotions, I suppose?' The words were out be-fore he could stop them. Old habits really did die hard.

She managed to keep her cool. After all, she'd felt dead inside for an age now. Since the last time she'd seen Jack, in fact.

'I wasn't given any choice in the matter. You bailed, remember?'

Jack was suddenly conscious of the poor choice he'd made in location for a declaration. He stepped closer, his voice low. 'Can we go outside for a minute?' He cleared his throat and forced out the word. 'Please?'

Her face remained impassive to his eyes while she thought, and Jack held his breath.

'Fine. For a minute. But that's all you're getting.'

It was still raining outside the hotel.

'I would just like to point out that it's raining out here.' Jack smiled hopefully as she turned to face him. 'Just in case you hadn't noticed.'

Tara was too busy noticing the number of women's faces appearing in the large windows beside them. She gritted her teeth against the cold. 'You really are a complete moron!'

Her anger surprised him. He frowned down at her. 'I'll give you a little leeway here, because technically you're probably right. But at least listen to what I have to say before you hit me with something again.' He waved at the windows without looking away from her face. 'Our audience deserves it, don't you think?'

'*Your* audience. Nothing to do with me!'

'Okay, then.' He smiled up at the windows, then glanced around the darkened street. His eyes searched for some privacy as he reached out to cup her elbow.

Tara shook her head again. 'Where do you think you're taking me, exactly? I have a writers' group to talk to, in case you hadn't noticed.'

'I'm well aware of the writers' group, thank you.' He tightened his hold when she threatened to snatch her arm away, steering her towards the large archways of an old abandoned cinema. Faded posters on the windows showed couples that appeared to be getting along much better than they were. He smiled wryly as he turned towards her. 'All I need is a few minutes.'

Managing to wrench her elbow from his grasp, she folded her arms across her chest and glared at him in the half-light. 'A minute was what you asked for and that's what you're getting. You've already *said* what you had to say. There is nothing else *to* say. What could you possibly say that would make a difference now?'

Jack looked upwards for a second, doing his best not to make a sarcastic retort, which would in turn lead to one of their famous sparring matches. Instead he managed to find patience before looking down into her sparkling eyes. 'I'm the kind of man you were talking about inside.'

'Now you think you're a hero?'

'With a little help I think I could certainly give it a try.'

'Oh, really?'

He frowned. 'Damn it, Tara, do you think this is easy for me?'

'I don't even know what *this* is!'

'It's a proposal, for crying out loud. Didn't you get that bit?'

Her grey eyes blinked up at him and her heart beat painfully against her ribs. She glanced away from his face to focus her attention on the fat raindrops that fell just beyond the archways. 'You've changed your tune, haven't you?'

'Yes, I have.' He stopped close in front of her, waiting until she looked up into his eyes. 'It turns out I was scared—by you, and by how I felt. So I ran.'

She felt tears well in the backs of her eyes.

'I was wrong.'

'You think?' Arms still crossed, she tucked her suddenly frozen fingers into fists, willing herself not to shiver. 'What happened to this all being too much for you?'

'It still pretty much is.' He smiled, ducking his head down as his voice dropped intimately. 'Which is why I need you.'

'You *need* me? You didn't need me a week ago.'

'Yes, I did. But that was too scary. Or so I thought. Thing is, I found something even scarier since then.' His eyes searched hers. 'I found out my life sucks without you in it.'

Her heart beat even harder, demanding that she listen to it for once. But Tara had already had that heart broken by Jack, and her mind really wasn't sure she could go through that again. 'And what happens when you get scared the next time? Or the time after that?'

He thought for several long moments before answering. 'I can't guarantee happily ever after. I'm sure there'll be just as many bad times as good.' He took a breath and reached out to rescue one set of frozen fingers from their hiding place. 'But I can tell you for a fact that I love you more than I ever thought I could love somebody, that I don't want a life without you in it, and that I'll try every day to look after you and be there for you.'

The tears threatened to break out from the corners of her eyes. She cleared her throat before asking, 'And if you can't?'

A small smile teased the corners of his mouth. 'If I can't then I'll have you to keep me on my toes and kick my ass back into shape.'

Tara looked away from his face and back at the rain. If she kept looking at him she'd give in before even thinking it through. It was already difficult enough not to just jump forward into his arms, what with the way his words had managed to reach out and ease her deepest fears.

Jack watched her, hardly aware he was holding his breath until his lungs screamed for air. 'I thought I loved Sarah once. I asked her to marry me because I wanted a family of my own. But in the end I guess I realised that I didn't want that family with just anyone. It had to be with the right someone.'

Her eyes remained fixed on the falling rain. 'And now you think that someone is me?'

'Yes.' The word was spoken with determination. 'I do.'

She blinked and blinked at the rain. Surely his declaration should have been enough for her? It was certainly fit to grace the pages of any book she'd ever written, any romantic proposal she could have dreamt of. Her hero. In the flesh.

With a small smile of irony she realised it was too much. Jack's exact words. *Too much.* She was still raw from the pain of his previous rejection—what if he changed his mind again? The answer was simple. She wouldn't survive it. Because, no matter how much he might irritate her, tease her, challenge her or in the end love her, it might not be enough to hold them together. The pain was already too much.

She shook her head, then summoned the courage to look back at him.

'Maybe if you'd said all this a week ago it would have made a difference.' She pulled her hand from the warmth of his. 'I've spent my whole life avoiding meeting someone like you, Jack. I never knew why, not really. I do now. I'm sorry, I just can't do this. I'm not strong enough.'

She turned and walked back into the rain, her shoulders hunched against the chill that filled her body.

Jack watched her walking away again. When she hunched her slight shoulders and reached a hand up to brush at her cheek it was all the sign he needed. In four long running steps he blocked her way. 'Oh, no, you don't.'

She blinked up at him, rain mixing with the tears on her face. 'Go away, Jack.'

'No.'

'What do you mean, no? I've given you my answer.'

He shrugged his rain-soaked shoulders. 'I'm not accepting that answer.'

'You have no choice.' She stared up at him incredulously. 'What are you going to do? Force me to marry you?'

'If that's what it takes, yes.'

'You can't do that. Even if you get me to the altar I'm still going to say no.'

He ignored the anger in her voice. 'When I get you to the altar you'll say yes, Tara Devlin. You'll say yes because you love me. Go on then.' He folded his arms in an exact mimic of her earlier stance. 'Deny it.'

'Right now I hate your guts!' She pushed him as hard as she could, both of her small hands against his chest.

It didn't move him an inch; instead he actually had the gall to smile. 'Flipside of the same thing, I'd guess.'

She screamed in frustration. It had been a long time coming—since she'd met him, in fact. 'How *dare* you? How dare you tell me how I feel?'

He stepped forward, hauled her into his arms and kissed her until she was breathless. 'I dare because I have no choice.' He lifted one hand to brush the damp hair back from her face. His voice softened again. 'Because if I'm wrong and you don't love me then I have to spend the rest of my life knowing I lost the only one for me, and I'm way too chicken to do that.'

Her breath caught on a sob.

He continued to run his fingers along the side of her cheek. 'Don't do that to me, Tara.' He leaned in and brushed his mouth across hers again before whispering, 'You'd have my suffering on your conscience for a long, long time.'

'You love me?' She blinked up at his face, inches from her own.

He smiled. 'Yes, I do.'

'You're really sure you're *in* love with me?'

He nodded. 'Yep.'

'And that I'm in love with you?'

His nod became more exaggerated. 'Yes, you are.'

Her large eyes continued to blink up at him. Then she noted the small flicker of doubt that crossed his face when she didn't speak. It was that flash of vulnerability that did her in. Because it echoed a part of herself. The part she'd managed to keep anyone from getting close to. Until there was Jack.

'Why in God's name did you come to a writers' group to tell me all this?'

He grinned. 'I thought the least a romance writer like yourself deserved was a grand romantic gesture. Heroic of me, huh?'

She shook her head. 'I didn't need some big heroic gesture, Jack. Telling me you love me would have done it.'

'Correct me if I'm wrong—'

'Don't I always?'

'Yes.' He grinned again, like the proverbial cat. 'Indeed you do. But didn't my telling you I love you very nearly *not* do it?'

She shrugged as a smile started in her eyes. 'Oh, I'd have believed you eventually—if you'd just continued telling me often enough…'

Pulling her closer, he leaned down to whisper, 'How about I just tell you every day for the next fifty or sixty years?'